RUMINATIONS

stories, essays & poems

RUMINATIONS
stories, essays & poems
By James Garrison
Published by TouchPoint Press
www.touchpointpress.com

Softcover ISBN: 978-1-956851-68-7

Editor: Kimberly Coghlan
Front Cover Design: Geoff Garrison
Cover Layout: Sheri Williams
Cover images: James Garrison
Interior Photos: ©James Garrison

Visit the author's website at https://jamesgarrison-author.com

@jamesgarrisonauthor @JimGarrison10 @garrijd

First Edition

Library of Congress Control Number: On File

Printed in the United States of America.

For my father and mother, without whom I would not be here, nor would I be who I am or lived the good life I've lived.

CONTENTS

STORIES
AND
ESSAYS

WHY I WRITE
(OR THE HOUSE MY FATHER BUILT)

What if . . .?

These are magical words. They can conjure new worlds—or at least different versions of the one you're in.

For years after I arrived home from Vietnam on a cold, gray Christmas morning, I avoided everything about Vietnam, reading, seeing, re-engaging in any way with my experiences there, although images would crop up every now and then, including in dreams in the wee hours of the morning, going back for another tour of duty, receiving my new jungle fatigues and boots and walking down the plane's ramp into the oppressive heat and humidity and strange odors of a foreign land.

Near the end of my legal career, my son asked me what I did in the war (or something like that), and I cynically told him that I specialized in brains—scrambled, sprayed, and over easy. He turned the soliloquy, which he recorded, into an art piece for his senior project at The Cooper Union—using a nice video of waves gently breaking on a beach in bright sunlight as background. Later, after I gave up "The Law," he challenged me to write a novel about it, about the things I had told him.

How do you write about something that happened years ago—something you'd just as soon forget? The images are still there, seared into the synapse, but what is the story that hasn't been told? Good, even great novels have been written about the Vietnam War: *The Things They Carried*, *Matterhorn*, and there are the movies like *Full Metal Jacket*.

And books by soldiers on the other side. But, I thought, there's another story. There's a story of the non-heroes, the common soldiers from all walks of life who did nothing particularly notable or heroic but still served honorably. And there is the inevitable corruption of war and the clash of cultures and peoples when one is wealthy, and the other is not. There was all the racial conflict and turmoil of the 1960s. What if . . .?

That was the genesis of my first novel *QL 4*.

•   •   •

I grew up in small-town Piedmont North Carolina in the 1950s and 60s, in a setting that seemed idyllic but wasn't in many ways for many people. In my working-class background, there was little that augured a future of writing anything, much less a novel (and reams of legal folderol). My mother dropped out of school after the first grade, she said, and my father quit after the fifth grade. They read the Bible and newspapers (my mother moving her finger across the page and mouthing the words), but no books. Except I *do* remember my father reading to me from two books before I started grade school, one about pilot Jack Knight and the other a musty volume we never finished. I can still visualize the faded image on the cover: a little girl, a scarecrow, and you know the others. For years, I wondered how it ended, until I read it to my own children. Or maybe I saw the movie first.

My road to writing was uncertain and torturous: a chaotic and sometimes bizarre family life—and a summer spent recovering from rheumatic fever, library books stacked around me on the bed and floor. Like many others who feel compelled to write, I lived, and live, in multiple worlds. There is, of course, the world of reality, a world of the senses perceived and interpreted by neurons and synapses, a world that is sometimes tragic, sometimes gloriously wonderful, and all the nuances in between. There's the world of absorbed knowledge from books and experience, from Plato to Madame Bovary to Einstein, and blood freshly flowing from a boy's wounds or glistening black on a floor, drained from a suicide's head. And there's the world of imagination, to which I escaped as a child, fleeing the house with my dog when my mother raged against my father over supper or fell into long fits of crying that led to a hospital gurney and electric-shock treatments. Imagination: the only place to which I could escape when I was thirteen, and on a snowy evening, animal-control took away my dog, a collie that looked like Lassie, only eight months old, because he was sick, perhaps with distemper, and my father couldn't, or wouldn't, afford the cost of vaccinations or a vet to treat him.

Eventually, if you discover this vast and mysterious new world of imagination, you want to explore it, to share it, to write about what you find there. What you can create from it. You become compelled to write about it. At least, I was.

On Friday, November 22, 1963, I was working in the shoe department of Belk's Bargain Basement, the evening shift after school, and no one was shopping. So I wrote the first essay I'd ever written that wasn't required by some teacher. I wrote it on the back of a white paper shopping bag. I had to write it. I had stayed up listening to the returns the night John Kennedy was elected president, to hear the final returns from Illinois, my father telling me to go to bed (he didn't vote because Kennedy was Catholic, but my mother did, for Kennedy). I'd followed everything Kennedy did in office, and I knew he and Bobby Kennedy were right about civil rights, despite my deep-rooted Southern heritage and everything I saw around me, the segregated schools, the theater, the water fountains, the swimming pool. The busload of teens from Jackson, Mississippi, at the Methodist Church camp the summer before, chanting, "We got a rope, we got a tree, all we need now is a Ken-ne-dy." I still have what I wrote, which on the torn bag unfolds over a foot long.

It was unjust, what happened to Kennedy; it was unjust what was happening all around me; it was unjust the centuries of mistreatment of human beings who differed from me only in the color of their skin, and I had to write about it. I still have to write about it. And the other manifold injustices in the world.

The Vietnam War, from the way it was prosecuted through its aftermath, was a grave injustice for many people, at many levels, and from many different perspectives. It seems now that most Americans just want to forget about it and ignore its lessons. I don't.

Of course, there are other reasons to write, some hidden deep in the subconscious, some far more worldly. One reason, an important one, is simply to entertain. With her solid first-grade education and powers of observation and vivid description, my mother was the storyteller of the family. But that's another story. A long one.

At the end of the day, I write because I'm at war with my own ultimate mortality.

Our father was a good man. That's what my brother said in the hospital corridor as he pulled out a package of Kents and offered me a cigarette. He made many sacrifices for our family, and he suffered much, with having to leave school and go to work in the furniture factory at fifteen and then three of his siblings dying untimely, violent deaths. Stoic, autocratic, reticent, my father was a mystery to me in many ways. After he died, when I was fifteen, I searched for anything he had written, anything anywhere he had put down his thoughts, so I could have something more than the memories, something that would replace the conversations I would never have with him as I grew older. All I could find was a pocket-size notepad he always carried, with some lists, groceries and the like. There may have been a note to my brother in college, sending a check. Years later, my Uncle John gave me a short letter my father had written to a shipmate of my Uncle Jim's, asking if he could visit the shipmate to talk about Jim's last moments. Both were on a destroyer that went down off Newfoundland in February 1942. The shipmate returned the letter to my Uncle John long after my father's death, along with the special delivery envelope. The only surprise in the letter was that my father would pay extra for special delivery.

But my father also built the house where I grew up. It's in the photo: white stucco, dark green roof, red brick chimney for a fireplace we never used. He dug the foundation and cellar, framed it in, laid the cinder blocks, applied the stucco inside and outside (the paint sometimes peeled off the walls in the winter cold, but it was cool like an adobe house in the summer), installed all the plumbing and electricity, and white-washed the outside almost every year. A few friends who also worked at the local Post Office where he worked doing maintenance—along with cleaning the toilets and polishing the spittoons in the Federal courtroom—helped him occasionally, my brother says.

My father left almost nothing in writing, but he built a solid structure that still stands after more than seventy years: a house that provides shelter and warmth to another family, as it did for ours. I could never build a house; I couldn't even square a board to build a birdhouse in eighth-grade shop. In my home office, I also have a platform rocker he made when he worked in the local chair factory in the 1930s. And I think of my father when I sit in the rocker and stare out the window at the leaves of the oak tree next to it.

So, this also is why I write, to create an edifice of words to memorialize what I've learned in life and to leave something behind for someone to read when I am gone.

THE OUTPOST

Just the three of them remained in the outpost: Pierre, the sergeant, Andre, the new guy from the capital, and Joe, the American. Then Pierre schlepped in the girl from the village. Slight, long black hair, olive skin, no more than sixteen, a native girl Pierre said he had been eyeing since his second week there.

They had been left behind to signal if the Majdi followed the retreating army (a strategic redeployment the captain called it) and marched on the capital—though they knew that the Majdi did not march; his men flowed like the first fingers of an incoming tide, slipping silently around rocks and dunes and along crevasses. These three soldiers were the captain's eyes and ears in the great, gray barrens of rock and sand, making their reports over a battered transmitter, alone in an abandoned stone fort on a promontory overlooking the desert.

There were still lights in the capital. From their high outpost, they could see the glow at night, just on the horizon, many miles in the distance.

They would remain for only twenty-four hours more. The retreating army would be in place and secure by then, not exposed to attack in the vast wilderness. For their escape, the captain had given them a good jeep and enough water and fuel to reach the capital. Two other jeeps were also there. Discarded from a prior war, they stood in the mid-stages of decrepitude on the slope below the fort.

So they had fuel and spare parts and enough water to make their exit when the time came—except for the girl, whom they would have to leave behind. That was unfortunate, Pierre said, since the Majdi's men would use her according to their custom and dispose of her as the offal of infidels.

The place itself was bleak, desolate. Andre, in his fresh uniform, his nostrils still tingling from the ocean air, had felt the contrast the minute he debarked from the plane and started up the escarpment. He felt it in all his senses: in the soughing of the wind and in the fine grains of sand that entered his eyes and nose and mouth and sought out every opening in his skin. He felt the absence of water and the fear of unquenched thirst. But most of all, he felt the desolation of the mind, the loss of hope, and the estrangement from those around him. Except, later, the girl. She had smiled shyly at him from the shadows of her shawl, and he wondered at her modesty—despite Pierre, whose porcine grunting came nightly from inside the cave-like fort.

From the first, Joe the American had not trusted Andre, that Andre could discern human form from shadows should the Majdi's men slink among the rocks below or up the steep cliff. Joe had not slept for days, instead keeping watch from the lookout post above the fort even when Andre was there. No one would sneak up on him—not Joe, seasoned veteran of the wars. The will to live oozed from Joe's pores, along with his sour sweat and a fear of death, mingling with the scent of contraband alcohol that came with each breath. But Joe rarely opened his mouth to speak, and never to say what he thought about the war, about their fate here in the desert.

Pierre, on the other hand, talked and talked and talked. That is, when he was not sleeping or rutting or filling his mouth with stolen meat from the village or the outdated American rations they had to eat and sputtering out flecks of food across the wooden table onto Andre's letter—dark spittle blotting "Cherie" and "t'aime," causing Andre to ball up the paper and toss it aside, then move to sit against a boulder, where he started over with a clean sheet resting on a month-old copy of *Le Monde*. That had been the night before the jeep.

Pierre was not afraid to die. He said so every two or three hours, when he was not rutting or sleeping.

Andre had known fear from the start. From the moment he had landed in this place. Even more from the moment the others had left, leaving him here with these two demented cast-offs and the girl. He knew it when he looked out at the blood-red sun sinking behind the empty horizon, and he worried about what it was that had led the captain to leave him in such company.

The desert contained many shades but few colors. At midday, it was almost blindingly white. In the slanting sun, it was gray with dark opaque shadows like a faded chiaroscuro landscape. And at night, once the last sliver of moon had glided into the west, it was black, eternally and profoundly black. Even the stars, like speckled ice, could not dispel it. Only the distant glow of the capital, forming a thin bowl on the horizon far to their rear, seemed to pulse with promise. After the curfew, even that light went out.

Andre, waking and feeling his rifle under his deadened arm, looked up and imagined smoke from burning buildings, yet he smelled nothing but the desert air, cool and stale. Some days the sky was crystalline blue, like the sky in a Renaissance painting he had seen in the Louvre, but now, on this, their last day, it was watery milk and the sun a faint moon-like orb wading through the murky reaches of space. Then he remembered what Pierre had done with the jeep, and the heavens seemed to close in on him like the lid of a coffin.

The girl had disappeared while Pierre slept, and he roused in a fury, ranting at Andre that it was his fault for letting her go. And so it was, because it was Andre who had been on watch, and he made no move to stop her when she ran from the fort, going on naked feet across the talus in the early morning light. Pierre had taken the good jeep and raged off along the rutted track to the village. When he returned, a boiling plume of dust and smoke followed the jeep, and its tires were shredded. But the girl was beside him.

All he would say—the old hags had set a trap, but he had fooled them. One old crone he had knocked silly and left lying in the dirt by the well. Probably the girl's grandmother or aunt or something. Her mother was dead in the war.

The girl kept her head down, looking at the ground from under her shawl as he talked. Andre's eyes stayed on her. Avoiding Pierre's harsh glare and unspoken rebuke.

Joe prowled around the smoking jeep and growled under his breath until he finally growled at Pierre: Why didn't you let the girl go? She hates you.

Pierre growled back that he had saved her; she was as good as dead back there.

Didn't she go on her own? Andre asked.

She was crazy, Pierre snapped. She was going to kill herself. He could not let such a pretty bird fly into the net. A tame one at that. He grinned a yellow-tooth grin above his loose double chin.

Andre thought, *He really means it.*

The girl leaned against Pierre and held his arm. See, Pierre said. She doesn't want to die. Not really.

So how do we get out of here? spat Joe. Now that you've fucked up the only good jeep we got. And we can't take her. We have to bring the ammo and guns and rations; we can't leave anything for the Majdi.

Burn it, said Pierre. And I can fix that one. He pointed to a rusting hulk with four intact tires down the slope. A relic from the last war.

Shit, shit, shit, said Joe.

Andre was quiet, not believing Pierre could fix anything.

But Pierre stashed the girl inside the stone fort and went to work on the old wreck, going back and forth between it and the smoking jeep that had been their salvation from this place, pouring precious water over the engine until it no longer smoldered.

Hours passed, and the sun left them, and the night came, but Pierre continued to work. Still, no sound came from the relic's engine, and finally Andre had slept, to awake to the milky sky, the silence, and the memory that living depended on Pierre fixing the relic.

While Joe stood guard, Andre tried to help Pierre with the jeep. The girl came out of the fort to sit on a granite boulder and watch them, and Pierre did not send her back inside. As the sun rose and the day grew hot, the shawl slipped from the girl's hair and her long skirt edged up her bare legs.

Now, Andre thought, *she has abandoned all shame and hope, and it does not matter to her anymore; nothing matters.* She ignored Pierre, but she smiled at Andre, who was closer to her age and not as ugly.

Andre offered her water and some chocolate from his rations, bringing a hissed rebuke from Pierre in her language. She snapped back at him in the same way and took the chocolate in a quick motion, saying *merci* to Andre. Touching his hand and smiling up at him.

Pierre glared at him, then told him, Go relieve Joe. As Andre trudged up the hill, he could hear Pierre banging on the engine and cursing it, trying to will it to start, while the girl watched.

It was good that Andre went. Joe had found a bottle of Cognac, and he was nursing it down with the help of a canteen of water and singing softly to himself, some dirge about rain. A rations box lay open in the gritty sand, its contents spread haphazardly about—except for the cigarettes, one of which hung limply from Joe's mouth. A thin streamer of smoke curled upward against a matching white sky.

Joe snuffed out his cigarette, grunted something in English, and then crawled to the far end of the trench, contorting his body like a snake to avoid spilling even a drop of Cognac. He closed his eyes and slept.

Andre held vigil over the dull shadows cast by a blurred sun until the shadows sharpened, shifted, and faded into the afternoon. He thought of the girl, the time he had seen her remove her black shawl and wash her olive arms. Her mother had killed a goat, slitting its throat with a knife and draining the blood into a pan. Nothing would be wasted, Pierre said; every ounce of the butchered animal would be saved and used, even the blood. A little was put aside for ritual, and the mother, now dead, had taken a finger and applied a small streak to the girl's forehead while the goat still quivered beside them.

After the butchering, the girl had gone to the well and drawn up the bucket. Removing her cloak and the shawl, she had washed her hands and arms and the blood from her face, not only the streak on her forehead, but also splatters on her cheek and neck. She did not have to worry about being seen because all the men were gone, either off with the Majdi or scouting for the captain. But Andre and Pierre had watched through binoculars from the hill above. That was when Pierre declared that she was his girl, and Andre had not believed him.

Andre started from his reverie. Sometimes he only imagined shapes below, but now he was certain a form had slipped between two large boulders on the lee side of the promontory. Hefting his rifle, he squeezed off three shots, like planed slabs of wood slapping together—bringing a spray of gravel from one of the boulders. But no response or movement. If there had been any before. Only an echo and a high, twanging whine as the bullets ricocheted among the rocks.

Joe jumped up, eyes wide, flinging his arms out and swinging his head around. Nothing else animate appearing, only Andre with a rifle pointed at the barrens below, Joe cursed both him and the desert, then settled like a weary old dog back onto his rocky bed. He drifted away again, the bottle cradled in one arm.

Andre returned to his vigil, watching the shadows spread like spilled honey over the desert floor. His eyes burned, his neck grew stiff, and sweat ran down his back and in rivulets under his arms.

The sun disappeared into the folds of dark clouds, and Joe roused once more and surveyed the sky. Sandstorm, he grunted, sitting up and stretching.

Andre lifted his rifle from the rough stone ledge of the parapet and slid down into the trench. Going to eat, he told Joe. You watch. He reached over and snatched away the bottle. You don't need this.

Joe mumbled a protest and shook his head, showing white stubble running halfway down his wrinkled neck and over his Adam's apple. He rolled to one side and, struggling to his hands and knees, crawled up the incline to the observation post.

Sandstorm, Joe said again and shielded his eyes to examine the horizon, where the sun had been swallowed by the gloom at the end of its arc. If we're lucky, it'll blow south. If we're not . . . He didn't finish.

Andre shrugged and left, rifle in one hand, Joe's bottle in the other. A storm would make it easier for the Majdi to invest the outpost in the night. But it could also cover their escape.

One more night, one last report, then destroy the transmitter and the fuel and the weapons they were leaving behind. And the girl? Andre groaned.

If only Pierre could get the jeep running.

Where was Pierre? Andre had heard nothing from him in the last hour. Not even a howled curse or the clanging of the wrench against metal.

From the path winding down the steep slope from the lookout, he could not see the jeeps or Pierre. All he could see were an array of boulders and the chiseled cliff behind the fort, rising above it like an ancient monument, shielding the outpost's farthest reaches with bleak shadows even until midday.

Doubt—and fear curdled in his throat. Perhaps they were overconfident of this promontory, pointed like a vast ship's prow out over the desert, its stern wedged against the sheer wall of towering rock. It would be a Herculean challenge to scale those walls or to sneak up the escarpment from the boulder-strewn desert below and then creep past the barricades and tripwires for the mines. But he was convinced that the Majdi's assassins would try. If they knew the three of them were still there, they would try. It was only within the womb-like interior of the stone fort that he felt safe.

Andre halted at a room-size boulder near the fort's entrance and surveyed the promontory out to the perimeter. Where the hell was Pierre?

Down the slope sat the relic, its bonnet raised. The jeep intended for their escape, now inoperable with shredded tires and a blackened engine, stood watch beside it. But neither Pierre nor the girl was in sight. Probably on Pierre's dirty mat inside the fort. And the relic had not started—he knew it had not because he had not heard it.

He dropped his steel canteen onto a warped gray plank that served as a table and felt the blackened can on the small G.I. pocket stove. Cold. Pierre had not rehydrated the dried meat he had taken from the village. Add water, and *voila*, a real meal—if you only had potatoes, red wine, and maybe some carrots and an onion. And rosemary. But the stove was cold and the cooking tin empty. He sighed. He'd have to use the last of his rations.

They were inside, and so were Pierre and the girl.

Leaning his rifle against the boulder, he removed his kepi and ran his fingers through his hair. He sat on a flat stone and laid his hat on the table, top down. Then he drank water from his canteen and stared at the sky. He drew circles in the dust at his feet and thought, measuring and weighing the years of his life, then weighing the odds of their extension— and hoping that Pierre and the girl would come out. Until finally, the twisting fist of hunger drove him inside.

Edging through the dark entrance, he felt his way to the alcove where his sleeping pad was stretched out on the stone floor and his few belongings were stashed along the back and on a ledge above. Once his eyes adjusted to the diffuse light from the entrance, he located the last of his rations and started out. Unable to resist, curious at the profound stillness, he glanced at Pierre's bedding. No Pierre, no girl.

He shuddered. No Pierre here, and silence outside.

Perhaps he had fled. But how? The dead jeep and the rusting relic he had been working on were still there.

Quickly, quietly, Andre slipped back outside. Placing his rations on the makeshift table, he picked up the rifle and pulled the bolt back for reassurance that a round was chambered. He checked the pistol on his belt, then paused to look up at the sky as if searching for an omen. Finding none, he started toward the jeeps, his hand squeezing the wooden stock of the rifle, a finger caressing the trigger.

He moved in a crouch. Swinging the rifle side-to-side, pivoting around to check behind him, he searched for any movement, anything new or strange on the boulder-strewn slope. From twenty yards away, he saw a pool of black liquid in a depression by the side of the relic. Then he saw Pierre, legs wedged under the dash, head back, a deep black gash where his throat should have been, and a dark bib on his pale, naked chest.

Andre's mind raced; his hands shook, but he was drawn nearer until he stared into Pierre's open eyes, fixed on a sky that had turned from milky white to dark gray. Andre's eyes darted about, taking in the points of the compass, heaven and earth. He expected to see the girl, like Pierre, her soft olive throat . . . And finally, he did see her. In a heap between two small boulders.

His eyes searched for the assassin. Fearing, anticipating, expecting the robed figure to jump out at him, the curved dagger aimed at his throat.

Backpedaling and turning, he scrambled up the slope toward the fort—but reversed himself when he heard a low moan. Running back, rifle in one hand, he reached the girl and pulled her up, searching for blood. Her black shawl had fallen onto her shoulders, and she looked up at him, her face contorted. Slowly she held out her hand, staring at it.

Blood.

He didn't see a wound. She must have touched Pierre, tried to stop the bleeding, perhaps. She really did care for him, he thought, for nasty old Pierre.

He did not think about Joe, that he had to warn him. He thought only about the girl and how fragile she looked.

She began to weep, and she tried to shake his hand away from her arm. He tugged at her then pulled her forward with him, almost dragging her, until they were huddled against the side of the fort. Leaning close to her face, he asked what happened—even though he knew already—what she had seen, even though he could visualize the robed figure going from boulder to boulder while Pierre fretted over the jeep and the girl dozed nearby.

Rien, she said and shook her head. She had seen nothing; then, she exclaimed some low guttural phrases in her own language. She wept.

Joe. He had to warn Joe. Even if it meant leaving the protected area in front of the fort where no one could sneak up on them.

It was almost dark now and the wind was up, filling his nostrils with a dry brackish smell that lingered as a taste in his mouth. As he started up the path, she called to him, not his name, which she had never used, but a plea of some sort in her own language, and he returned to her. She grasped his sleeve at the elbow and held up a hand, small and stained with Pierre's blood. He took his canteen from beside the table and poured water into the palm she held out to him in supplication, then with the loose end of her shawl, he wiped off Pierre's blood. It was not dry, but still sticky.

Forgetting Joe, he gave her water to drink and drank some himself. Thinking, *the same metal her mouth had just touched*. He opened the rations box and split its contents with her, only then realizing he was famished. She ate hungrily, and he also did—at first. Remembering Joe—and that one of the Majdi's warriors might be near—killed his hunger.

He ceased picking at the nameless meat and placed the open tin on the plank table. He took the girl by the elbow and raised her up, forcing her to abandon the food. Holding her arm, he steered her to just inside the fort's entrance. Stay here, he said, motioning with his hand stretched out. Use the torch if you need it, but only in an emergency. And stay inside.

He did not know if she understood, but she did not object.

Collecting his rifle and kepi, he hurried up the rock-strewn path with as much stealth and speed as he could manage in the all-encompassing night, only the dull glow of the capital on the horizon behind him to light his way. The wind had filled the air with fine grains of sand, and he had to clutch at his hat to keep it from flying away. The storm had not gone south.

When he reached the outlook, he called for Joe in a low voice.

No answer. And he didn't see Joe, not even the capital's reflected light on Joe's pale face. There was no sound, except the wind brushing sand along the ground and over the rocks.

He called again. No answer.

He lowered himself onto his hands and knees at the bottom of the trench and took a box of matches from his pocket. Shielding a match next to the ground, he struck it against the box and held it out. Crouched down, rifle across his bent legs, he twisted first to his left and, seeing nothing there, to his right. Joe. Slumped down as before, where he had been sleeping with his cradled bottle. Except now a long dark stain extended down the front of his tunic from his lowered chin to his crotch. Andre did not have to lift Joe's head or look into the face to see what had happened.

He glanced about in the flickering match light, fearful that the curved knife would come over *his* shoulder next and open *his* throat this time. Joe's canteen lay at the bottom of the trench, open, empty. The flame scorched his thumb; he dropped the match, and it flared out. Scrambling out of the trench, he ran down the path: stumbling and tripping and recovering again, holding onto his kepi, the rifle banging against his thigh.

The girl was outside, sitting with her back against a rock, her hands folded loosely in the lap of her long skirt. He plunged past her into the deeper darkness of the fort and seized the electric torch from a ledge. Playing the beam over the worn ground of the open plaza, he stopped it on the girl's face. She gave him a frightened look.

Now it was just him and the girl—and whoever was out there with the knife. Lurking inside the perimeter. And now, if the assassin had a pistol, he could shoot them both, and the noise would not matter because there was no one else to hear, to help. Just them, and they would be next.

They needed to escape this place. Slip into the defile at the back of the outpost and go across the desert to the capital. But they would never make it. It was three days on foot, and that was in decent weather.

The wind whistled among the rocks and flayed grit from the cliff above them. Sand stung his exposed face, even within this sheltered area. Damn Pierre and his jeeps.

Maybe the captain would send help. He laughed, a hoarse, desperate cough. But he tried the transmitter anyway. The switch was on, the batteries drained. A low buzz came from it, fainter and fainter as he pleaded into the microphone. Then nothing.

He had to leave, get out of this slaughter pen. But he couldn't leave the girl, so young, so helpless, at the mercy of the Majdi.

With the remaining water, he half-filled two canteens, then collected rations, ammo for the rifle, and two grenades. The rations and ammo he stuffed into a pack, and the grenades he clipped to his belt. One of the canteens he handed to the girl. Pressed it against her hands until she understood and took it.

We go, he said, pointing to the horizon. Despite the sand whipping around them, the lights in the capital still glowed, if only dimly. Hefting the pack onto his back, he slung the rifle over one shoulder and the canteen over the other, then seized the girl by the arm and drew her after him, into the fort. To a narrow recess at the rear, their escape route if they were overrun.

Releasing the girl, he placed the flashlight on the floor and used his full strength to roll aside a large mill-wheel-like stone, exposing a dark hole near the base of the cave's wall. Holding the light in one hand and pushing his rifle in front of him, he crawled through a short tunnel that debouched into an open defile formed by ancient floods. Once through and standing erect, he motioned with the light for the girl to follow. She hesitated, then understanding, scurried out to join him.

They made their way down the passage, Andre in front, feeling his way along the wall until it opened into a long, deep crevasse that stretched down to the desert floor. With no other guidance, he tugged the girl toward the faint glow on the horizon.

Bent against the wind, they struggled forward while the sand whipped their faces and pushed them at an angle away from the glow—until it, too, disappeared, either because of the curfew or the lowering clouds of airborne earth, leaving the horizon as black as the rest of their world. The sand surged around them, covering them with waves of dry grit, filling mouth and nose and ears, despite the girl's shawl and a towel he had wrapped around his head and face and neck. His kepi was long gone.

She stumbled as he tugged her along by the hand, and then he stumbled, too, and they both dropped onto a gravelly surface. A disjointed wall loomed before them. Together they crawled forward and into a small cave formed by giant boulders propped each against the other.

We wait here, Andre gasped, pulling the girl deeper into the depression under the boulders. Turning on the light, he swept it around. A scorpion, tail swaying in the air, ran across the girl's bare ankle and into an opening under one of the rocks. She gave a squeal of fright and huddled close to him, and he slipped one arm around her shoulders.

Inside the little cave, they did not feel the great blasts of wind or the sting of sand, and despite the place and the storm, Andre felt safe and comforted by the girl's dependence on him, her warmth under his arm.

Removing his pack, he placed the rifle to one side and drank some water from his canteen. He motioned for her to do the same, stopping her after only a swallow. They would need the water for the trek across the desert, tomorrow and the day after, and the day after. He despaired.

They lay down, apart from each other, and he dozed.

He awoke from a small movement near him, and he first thought of scorpions. But no. The girl had moved to lie beside him. The night was cold, and she nuzzled under his arm again. He touched her face, the smooth, warm skin, and he felt moisture on her cheek. Tears. He felt sad at her tears, losing everything and having to flee her village. He lay awake and thought—fantasies, of his life, of the girl—but then he remembered the journey. They would make it; he swore it. He would do it for her. For them.

The wind had ceased its howling, and a dull light appeared outside. Through the opening, he could see that the storm had subsided, though fine particles of sand remained suspended in the air.

He could see the girl's face now. Her eyes were closed, her pink lips pulled up in a faint smile as if she dreamed of something pleasant. Still gazing at her face, he fell asleep.

He awoke and felt her hand gently caressing his cheek, then his forehead, and her fingers running through his hair. Swinging one leg across his body, she straddled him. He gazed up, into her eyes, and he saw there only dark emptiness. She jerked his head back. In his remaining seconds, he realized that there were many things he did not know or understand, and that he did not have to worry about crossing the desert.

Fin

STRANGERS ON THE APPALACHIAN TRAIL

Over a long life, I've spent much time lost in my own mind while I wander alone—though my wife often joined me on many treks. It's always distressing to read that some mass murderer or other was a loner. As if Henry David Thoreau and John Muir were threats to society. Or perhaps they were.

On most occasions, I try to bend to the demands of social interaction and to listen and speak sensibly. At least when there's a glass of wine and toothpick-speared shrimp involved. Yet, I'd rather be on a long road to somewhere else or on a trail in the mountains of Colorado or North Carolina. Or watching a sunrise or sunset from a cabin deck, rain coming in a wave down a valley, or lightning in jagged streaks over the ocean at night. When I was ensconced in a corner office in downtown Houston, Texas, some of my best moments were spent staring out the window at the sun setting beyond the Galleria and the crenelated buildings breaking the horizon, a prism of colors flaring and fading into night as I thought of nothing but the display before me. These were probably some of my most productive minutes at work, certainly the most calming after a long day of chaos and conflict and wondering what I was doing there.

In my younger days, I thumbed over highways in North Carolina, often late at night: for dates at UNC-Greensboro (then called the Woman's College) because the faces I'd most like to see weren't in my classes in Chapel Hill, where we males outnumbered females four to one; or on a Saturday, I'd flee the campus and the town, as quaint and idyllic they might be—the campus now overrun by more students and the town no longer a village, the Rathskeller and Zoom-Zoom and Intimate Bookshop all long gone. Once a friend and I set out for an ocean beach near his hometown, our thumbs out, but we made no more than twenty miles and a six-pack of Michelob down a dark pine-flanked highway before turning back to study for exams, mine on Milton—alone on a sunny Sunday morning, leaning against an old oak tree on the quad, reading marked passages in "Paradise Lost" and only dreaming of warm sand and rolling waves and nubile coeds in bikinis. My friend, dying young and long dead now, his face and voice remembered, sitting under a streetlamp at a two-lane crossroads, popping the top on another beer.

Or later, thumbing rides to visit a girlfriend, already an ex and indifferent to my draftee plight, traveling miles and miles late into the night over rural Carolina highways from military training in Georgia . . . My point is you don't have to be stark raving mad or even a bit looney to go wandering by yourself to see the world or seek whatever it is you want to find, the Holy Grail or Dulcinea, or to escape whatever it is pursuing you. But sometimes it helps to be different and removed from the masses, marching to the beat of your own drummer, as they say.

Not long ago, just when the leaves were donning their fall colors, I did a few day-hikes on different segments of the Appalachian Trail in the Nantahala Mountains; I met almost no one along the way, coming or going, which suited me fine. Many hikers I have met in the past were interesting people with interesting stories to tell: a fresh-faced young woman hiking the entire trail, 2,100 miles or so, before her induction into the military (athletic, idealistic, dedicated), a young man who said it was best to hike wearing a kilt, though he did not, and the man who was wearing a kilt and as macho, big, and scruffy as any mountain man who went fur trapping with Jim Bridger or any burly Scotsman hunting the king's deer.

Trail sign on AT – Rock Gap

This fall day on the AT in western North Carolina, I met a kid (who said he was thirty, but he looked like a kid, a teenager) smoking a stub of a cigarette at Panther Gap, on a rise just above the trail, where through the trees you could see a wide blue valley and blue mountains in the distance.

He'd been on the trail for a couple of weeks he said and asked if he could hike along with me. He was by himself; the others he'd met on the trail were mostly day hikers and out of breath, and they all seemed to want to avoid him. I could see why. Shabbily dressed in a ragged shirt and torn jeans, he had a pale sunburned face, shag-cut brown hair and no hat, and more rings in his lower lip, nose, and ears than I could count, if I'd cared to try. His pack was crude, not like anything I'd ever seen a through hiker carrying, and what looked like a tarp for a tent, and no sleeping bag, all of it tied together with a thick, once-white rope, a tin cooking pot dangling on one side.

Certainly, I told him, you're more than welcome to hike with me. I'm only going to Siler Bald. But I made sure he was in front, just in case. I didn't want to be throttled from behind.

He was going to hike the whole trail, he said—and how many miles is that from south of the Smoky Mountains? And at ten or fifteen miles a day? Then I noticed he was wearing tennis shoes. And his worn blue jeans, faded to a fashionable white, had a rip in the back below one thigh.

As we walked, I heard his life story. Raised by his grandparents, both dead now of cancer. House he inherited near Houma, Louisiana, flooded out by a hurricane, one of those after Katrina. He gave the insurance money to his daughter, now living with an aunt, and he left to go wandering. He'd been all over: Arkansas, Tennessee, Georgia, Michigan, where he was robbed by a man who gave him a ride in his pickup truck and offered him a job and then at a service station, made off with all the kid's possessions. A few weeks later, another man bought him a bus ticket to Tennessee, where he worked as a handyman until the urge to hike took him again, and he hit the trail from Chattanooga. On a whim, when he was on the Rainbow Trail in Georgia, he said over his shoulder, he decided to do the Appalachian

Trail, and he had just started out from Springer Mountain—at the end of August.

I'm sure I told him a tale or two of my own, that I had written a novel set in the Mekong Delta in 1970 and I'd been a military cop there for a while. But I don't remember which stories I told him, just a couple from my repertory, mostly true ones or at least true in my mind.

We stopped to rest, and I shared some of my food with him, but he never asked for money, although just in case he did, I pulled a twenty out of my wallet when he couldn't see and palmed the folded bill into my front pocket. He was almost out of food, he said. Planned to replenish his supplies at the Nantahala Outdoor Center, he thought it was called, maybe a half day up the trail. I offered him some pumpernickel bread and sharp cheddar cheese from what I'd brought for my lunch—but in handing him the bread, I dropped the apple I was going to have for a snack. It tumbled down the slope, bouncing and rolling through wet leaves and ferns as I stared after it and said, ah shit! Raccoons or bears will enjoy that. But the stranger chased it down, plunging through the undergrowth and snagging it twenty feet below, not something I'd ever do short of near starvation. Climbing back up to the path, he offered me the apple, reaching out with it in one hand. No thanks, I said—not after it's rolled down a mountainside. If I didn't want it, he asked, could he have it? Okay, but I suggested he wash it off first with water from his bottle; but he just rubbed the apple on his dirty shirt, then bit deep into the fruit. I offered him a paper towel. And some more food.

The day before, on another section of the Appalachian Trail near Albert Mountain, I believe it was, I met a lovely English lady *d'une certaine age* who was attired as if out of the Arabian Nights and carrying a bright blue pack almost as big as she. She came over by ship, she said, specifically to hike the AT, by ship to reduce her carbon footprint a bit, and she'd started somewhere up north, New York perhaps, but I can't remember where. She wore a white tunic of some sort and filmy, pastel-blue pantaloons tied at her ankles just above sturdy brown hiking boots. All her life, she'd been hiking all over the world—and the AT was a trail she'd always wanted to do.

In her proper British accent, the English lady asked if she could share the log where I sat eating my lunch of black bread and cheddar cheese.

Shelter on AT where strangers meet

We stayed there for a while, side-by-side, the trees shading us from the midday sun, forest birds singing around us, and we talked of many things. She didn't tell me her life story or why she hiked, nor did I tell her my life story or why I hiked.

What we did talk about was the forest around us because it was new to her. Waving my free hand toward the treetops (the other held bread folded over a hunk of cheese), I told her about the similar sounds of robins and scarlet tanagers, the varied calls of the Carolina wren, and the mellifluous bell-like songs of the thrushes I could never tell apart, but my wife could. Along the trail were wildflowers and shrubs, sometimes in thick groves arching over the path; the only ones I knew were flame azaleas—bright-orange flowers sprinkled among the trees on the hillsides; mountain laurel and their Milky-Way clusters of white flowers all about us along the trail; gnarled thickets of rhododendron not yet in bloom, but later, in June, they would crown the path.

We agreed that it seemed warmer now in the fall than when we were young, and I asked if she had seen all the dead and fallen trees in places along the trail. The Carolina and eastern hemlocks, which used to shade the streams rushing down "v's" in the Nantahala hillsides, had been infested by insects, invasives to this continent; and the hemlocks had all died and rotted and fallen into tangled heaps just in the last few years. Years past, my wife and I ate lunches of bread and cheese by tumbling streams in the shade of hemlocks, but we would never be able to do that again. The same had happened to the American chestnut trees that once populated the forests throughout these mountains, well into the last century, and they all died, except for saplings that still spring up here and there but grow to less than my height, then die before growing into mature trees. Scientists were working on resurrecting the American chestnut, or so I read somewhere, and returning healthy stands of them to forests and towns. And maybe it would happen someday, but I doubted I'd live to see it. Still, we had the tall oaks, maples, and tulip poplars, like the ones around us, and perhaps they would survive in these ancient mountains for hundreds, even thousands of years into the future. Or perhaps not.

I noticed dark clouds gathering above the mountains across the valley and said I wanted to finish my hike before afternoon thunderstorms caught us there in the woods. She would linger a while in this sun-dimpled glade, she said, and so she did. I slipped on my daypack and binoculars and picked up my hiking stick, made from the spine of a saguaro cactus (a friend had given it to me), and left her there, sitting on the log we had shared.

She didn't pass me during the couple of miles I walked back down the mountain to Rock Gap and to my car parked below, but I wondered as I made my way around the rocks and roots in the trail if I should wait and offer her a ride into Franklin, where she planned to spend the night. I regretted I hadn't made the offer while we shared the log and talked and ate lunch. But sometimes you don't do what you should have done, and it's just an oversight. And then it's too late. I drove away.

As for the stranger who hiked with me to Siler Bald—I trudged far ahead of him in going up a steep section of the trail (climbing faster than the kid since I carried only a light pack, binoculars, and a liter of water), and then I climbed a long side trail to the bare-rock bald at over 5,000 feet. Topping the first crest in the side trail, I glanced back and saw the stranger enter a soccer-field-size meadow below. Snowbird gap or something like that, I think it was. He dropped his pack on the ground and stood, looking up after me.

Side trail to Siler Bald

Siler Bald summit view

It was midday when I started back down the trail, headed to Winding Stair gap where I'd started that morning and where the trail crossed the highway into Franklin. I would eat lunch, or what was left of it, at my favorite log in a copse of trees just off the trail a mile or so below.

We parted ways at Snowbird gap, the stranger and me. The last I saw of him, he lay stretched out in the grassy meadow, leaning against his pack and smoking one of his stubby cigarettes while staring up at a blue sky studded with cottony clouds. He'd only stopped to rest, he said, as I paused strolling past; he did not want to climb Siler Bald. This is what he loved, the open sky and the mountains around him. Entering the forest beyond the meadow, I called goodbye and good luck. He waved one hand in the air, a wispy stream of smoke drifting above his face.

Over my iPhone that evening, I told my wife about hiking with the kid—I forget his name—and we both laughed at him calling me a mountain goat for how fast I went up the hills at age 70. Then I described to my wife the panoramic view from Siler Bald, where we had hiked together in years past, and the beautiful sunset I could see from my cabin that evening.

Author's wife – at a favorite stop for lunch

And I wondered where my new friend had spent the night. And what he ate.

Along with a little food, I'd also given him some advice, to the extent I could. He should get off the trail, at least by Pennsylvania, before it gets icy cold. You can do Katahdin only in good weather, I told him, and the White Mountains are not a friendly place to be in the winter. Also, keep an eye on the trail and where you step. It's breeding season for snakes in the fall, at least I think it is. The timber rattlers, which I've seen a few times while hiking in the Nantahalas in September and October, are in their yellow phase and really pretty, with a contrasting black and yellow pattern all along their bodies down to the rattles; and for some reason they seem quite comfortable lying across the trail and not moving for human interlopers. But the ones we've seen in the past, my wife and I, give a nice signal that sounds like an old telephone when you get too close, into their claimed space. Just freeze and back off slowly. Though my wife enjoyed hearing the phone ring when she took a step forward and then backed off—before I urged the snake to let us pass with the end of a long stick. Meeting a rattler across the path, we usually slog around the obstinate reptile and make our own elliptical path up a slope away from the trail, through fall leaves that might conceal a copperhead, until we return to the worn human right-of-way—and look back to see the timber rattler moving off the trail of its own accord.

There are other dangers about which I did not warn him, other than be careful and keep your eyes open: bears and feral hogs, though they are easily avoided if you steer clear and carry a bear canister for food, which he did not, but he could hang his food from a high limb with his rope. Of the bears I'd encountered, none ever posed a threat. Except *one* in the Shenandoah Valley with two cubs, searching for food, and she tore up a car, claws hooked over the driver's window and pulling it outward, then climbing on the roof and sagging it in.

Sometimes there are hostile people, though I've never personally met any, but I've heard a few are out there with guns and knives. I did personally know the dangers of injury when you hike alone. On a loop trail around Standing Indian Mountain—only eleven miles and one of my favorites, I tripped over a root while coming down from the mountain top on a sun-washed afternoon and slammed my face into a flat rock, breaking my nose but not my glasses. Something I recalled from a book—a man straightened his own broken nose. And that's what I did, pulling it forward and down.

I walked out of the woods that day, down the AT to the side trail that delivered me to my car, four miles, stumbling along and pressing my sweatshirt to my face. I survived with a few antibiotics, bandages, and a couple of CAT scans, the only lasting effects a slightly crooked nose and an indentation where my glasses now fit snuggly. The next spring, I returned to the Standing Indian loop by myself (despite the doctor's admonition), and enjoyed the solitude more than ever, the bird songs, the spring greenery, and the canopies of flowering mountain laurel. Treading on quartz and mica grit scattered by thousands of boots and moccasins along an ancient Cherokee trading route, gazing at the blue mountains across the valley that beckoned me to reach out to them. A perfect day for a walk in the woods and a perfect setting for my daydreams.

I wonder if he kept at it, the stranger I met on the Appalachian Trail that fall day. And why he goes wandering alone on forest trails. He said he might stop hiking in five years or so, after he got the need to keep going out of his blood. I often wish I'd given him that twenty in my pocket so he could buy food at the Nantahala Outdoor Center. I doubt he starved, though I don't know how he could have continued much farther. Perhaps through the kindness of strangers. If you have no home, I guess the Appalachian Trail, or any trail through a wilderness, is as good a place to be as any, and better than most.

The End

THE POISONING

Through a printed window, I saw my forebears encapsulated in amber and pinned on a page, a pause in time captured and frozen in a news clipping of a death by poisoning deemed suspicious and meriting a formal inquest in rural North Carolina in 1888 and memorialized in statements written by educated others and signed with an "X" as his or her mark: the four children still at home (Ben, Em, Mary, and their half-brother, Sam), there with the old man, Smith Bell, when he died—and "the colored boy," Will, who they said stayed at the house during the day and ate the leftover food in the kitchen pots when the white family was done. He was the only one who didn't get sick and vomit his guts out two weeks before or again after breakfast the day the old man died, both times when they all were sick, except the "negro boy who lives here was not sick either time," according to the youngest son Sam's statement in the inquest.

This was August 1888 and Grover Cleveland was president. Reconstruction in the South was long past, ended ten years before, and all the blue-clad Federal troops withdrawn, leaving the Ku Klux Klan, white robes flying, rising from the ashes of defeat to restore the old balances of race and class and fear and maintain the established order for a desperate white society.

So how did it end, and equally curious, how did it start there on old Smith Bell's farm? All of them living together, farmers, not sharecroppers, the old man a blacksmith and a landowner, twice widowed, his grown sons going off to catch the horses before breakfast and then to plow the fields afterward and getting sick, and the old man dying like that, the father of Ben, Em, Mary, and Sam, and also the father of Thomas Smith Bell, my great-grandfather, whom I know only from a black-and-white photograph taken in his old age— long white beard and bib overalls, standing with five men and a boy from succeeding generations, all relatives of mine, in front of a makeshift sawmill, and who died in 1922, falling off the porch, stone dead, while my mother, age 10, watched and then told me about it fifty years later: my great-grandfather dropping dead before her eyes; how was it that his father came to die by poisoning in August 1888?

In his statement at the inquest: Benjamin Bell, age 27, after being duly sworn, says: "Our family consists of (or did) my father, one brother, two sisters & my self [sic.] & a black boy about 16 years old. We all stay here at night except the boy & he goes to a black mans [sic.] to sleep (Cal Allison)."

How did the six of them arrive here at this moment in time, together in old Smith Bell's house on an August morning in 1888? The 70-year-old father and four of his children by two dead wives and Will, "a black boy about 16 years old." Two older children—Lieuhanna and Thomas Smith Bell, my great-grandfather, who dropped dead and fell off the porch of a farmhouse in 1922 while my mother watched (and later held funerals and made a graveyard, she said, for all the birds and chickens who died in the yard)— had both gone off to start their own lives, still close by, working the same red-dirt farmland where the family had lived for a hundred years and more and where my mother grew up in a four-room farmhouse and chopped cotton instead of going to school when she was ten years old—and after, until she went to work at the shirt mill when she was fourteen.

Before the War (the only one that counted here in 1888), Smith Bell and his family did not have a plantation, only a farm, where one supposes they grew cotton for cash, corn for animal feed (and liquor), garden vegetables for the table, and peaches for the pie that Ben ate that morning for breakfast.

Before the War, one may ask with some misgivings, did old Smith Bell own slaves, perhaps the parents of Will. From a few surviving documents in an estate settlement, we know that circa 1850 Smith Bell inherited "one-half the value of Hannah, about 20 years of age—$700," the other half divided among the other heirs of Nancy Bell, his mother, also the first cousin of his father, not so unusual in those days, in small, close-knit communities.

How do you divide a person, or the value of a person? Was Hannah sold, and the proceeds allocated among the owners? Owners of another human person, with her own hopes and fears, and no freedom or say in what happens to her that day or the next.

According to county records, before the War old Smith Bell was sometimes a "patroller" in his "militia district," in other words, part of a "slave patrol" to keep the subject race in check and prevent insurrection. How is it that neither he nor anyone else in his immediate family served in the War? Where were they, and what were they doing while the armies of blue and gray surged across the land and thousands were dying of violence and disease? Were they older, younger, lamer, or just wiser than the others?

And why did Will, "a black boy," full name Will Allison, come to stay with the Bell family during the day in 1888? He ate alone, in the kitchen, the food the white folks left on the stove that last day old man Bell was alive, my great-great-grandfather, who, his daughter Em says, had only a cup of coffee for breakfast.

Foul play was suspected, and the coroner cut out the old man's stomach and sent it to the State Chemist in Raleigh for analysis of its contents. There was a headline in the local newspaper, **Statesville Landmark, August 16, 1888: "A Probable Poisoning."**

"There is every reason to suspect that poison was given the family," the article said. And who was suspected but Will. "With [the family] . . . lived a colored boy about 15 years old, who spent the night at the house of his grandfather, . . . [and he] was not taken sick either time when the white members of the family were. He always ate in the kitchen, his meals being left in the vessels in which the cooking was done." What capped off Will as the prime suspect was that "Neither he [Mr. Bell] nor his family had any enemies, so far as they or any of their neighbors know."

So there it is, in rural North Carolina in 1888, in the trusted local newspaper, the finger of suspicion pointed at Will, "a colored boy about 15 years old." Was Will interrogated, threatened, whipped? Held in the county jail? What kind of life did he have after that? Did the local chapter of the Ku Klux Klan or some random lynching party show up at his grandfather's house? Did he flee?

The day after old man Bell died, Will appeared at the inquest. I wonder where it was held, perhaps at the family home, the old man's decaying body in a wooden coffin in the next room, the coroner and jury sitting in straight-back chairs around the dining room table, the children and Will talking as the scribe wrote out their statements and they signed with an "X" in the middle of their written name.

Will says in his written testimony: "I live here, have been here a year & a half. Eat here but sleep down at grand paps." He admits he did not get sick the day the old man died or two weeks before when all the others were sick. Will says, "[I] was not here yesterday morning until the boys were catching the horses and then ate my breakfast, ate three biscuits and some butter, did not have any coffee, don't drink it in the summer."

Em says that the only thing the old man had for breakfast was a cup of coffee.

It was August 9, 1888.

Benjamin, Emily, Mary, and Sam lived long lives, remained close to their old homestead and the land their family had held onto and farmed for generations. Thomas Smith Bell, Smith Bell's oldest son and my great-grandfather, was not a blacksmith. He continued to farm nearby and, in his later years, had an unfortunate encounter with a train that severed a heel, my mother said, so that he walked on the ball of his foot. HE WAS NOT DRUNK is reported in the family history. What happened to the mule and wagon is not reported.

As to old Smith Bell, my great-grandfather's father, the coroner's jury of "six good and lawful men" concluded that "the deceased came to his death under very suspicious circumstances & by some unknown causes to us." The two doctors who conducted a postmortem examination found that it "did not clearly reveal to us that he was poisoned since we have not examined the contents of his stomach." They reserved their final opinion "until such examination should be made as prescribed by law."

Sam Bell, the youngest son at age 24, being sworn, says at the end of his statement in the inquest: "I do not suspect any person of poisoning us."

Many months later, there was an answer to one of the questions, or so it seems: **"NOT a case of poisoning—a satisfactory explanation"** is the heading of an article in the **Statesville Landmark, May 23, 1889**. "It will be remembered that about the first of August last year," so the article begins; it then recapitulates old man Bell's death "under circumstances which suggested poisoning. A small colored boy who lived with the family was suspected." But the long-awaited report by the State Chemist in Raleigh concluded that: "[A]fter an extended examination for all classes of poisons I have not found any substance of a poisonous nature . . . It is possible that the symptoms observed may have been due to the peculiar class of ptomaine compounds which are not thoroughly understood—possibly to some substance resembling tyrotoxicon, which owes its origin to putrefactive matter in meats, milk or vegetables. The symptoms for tyrotoxicon poisoning seem to resemble those observed in the case of T. Smith Bell."

So in 1889, in post-Reconstruction North Carolina, on the cusp of Edison's lights and another Bell's telephone, there was a victory for science and justice even if the odor of foul murder had lingered in the air for a long nine months. The State Chemist's letter to the Board of County Commissioners goes on to justify his delay in conducting the analysis and sending the report by the press of other business, including the responsibility of the State Chemist for analyzing fertilizers, an issue "in which the farmers of the State are interested to the amount of millions of dollars."

Who knew that fertilizer was so important to the farm economy in North Carolina in 1888? Certainly not I. But it was. After the War, by 1888, the production of cash crops like cotton and tobacco, along with farm animals, had returned to pre-War levels, but the farmers' incomes had not.[*] There was over production, nationally and locally, and commodity prices were severely depressed in the years since 1865, cotton dropping "from 25 cents a pound in 1868 to . . . 9 cents in the 1880's" while the farmers' expenses for machinery, fertilizer, and freight rates had declined little or not at all. Farm tenancy and crop liens were on the rise. Farm income was depressed not only by costs but also by a monetary policy that deflated the wages of labor along with the prices of cotton and other fruits of the land, to the ultimate benefit of the lenders, railroads, and robber barons—and led to William Jennings

---

[*] See *North Carolina*, Lefler and Newsome (The University of North Carolina Press 1963) pp. 490-493. This is the text we used in a North Carolina history course at the state university in 1964. In another first-year class, Western Civilization I believe it was called, the professor announced on the very first day: "The WAR is over! And you lost." That made sense to me, based on what I knew then, but I'm not sure it did to everyone there, fifty or so students, most from North Carolina, assembled in a large auditorium for the mandatory course.

Bryans' call to arms: "you shall not crucify mankind on a cross of gold."

Around them the farmers could see the manufacturers, bankers, and urban professionals prospering while they did not. "In 1890 the wealthiest three percent of the American population owned sixty-five percent of the national wealth while the poorest eighty-seven percent owned only ten percent."[*] So the farmers went deeper in debt and struggled to make crops grow on tired land that, in the absence of Twentieth-century farm technology and knowledge, required ever more fertilizer each year. They were squeezed and bled by bankers, manufacturers, and politicians who raised taxes on their land and crops. And they organized granges and alliances to make their voices heard and their votes count. So in North Carolina, a farm state, fertilizer was extremely important to the farmers, and the farmers to the politicians and the State Chemist.

But what about Will, whose fate hung in the balance because fertilizer was more important to the State Chemist? What happened to Will, the "small colored boy who lived with the family"? What became of him during all of this, during the nine months it took for the report to be concluded and sent to the Iredell County Commissioners: "NOT a case of poisoning"?

Could this be the same Will Allison who appears in the county census records of 1900, the Will Allison who has his own story and family history? And his descendants, progeny of slaves, still compelled to struggle against the grasping tendrils of American slavery and Jim Crow; where are they now? Chicago, Los Angeles? Or still tied to the land, the red-dirt soil and rolling hills of Piedmont North Carolina, like many of Thomas Smith Bell's descendants.

---

[*] Lefler and Newsome, p. 493.

Perhaps none of this matters, only the present moment, while the past remains forever fixed in time, frozen in amber, and rarely remembered.

Acknowledgments: With special thanks to R.C. and Irene Clanton Black for sharing their research into the Bell family history along with copies of the news clippings from the *Statesville Landmark* and documents from the coroner's inquest into the death of Thomas Smith Bell, who died on August 9, 1888.

FAT JULIET

THIS TIME Chi channeled a cat. Usually it was humans, but why not a cat? No impediments to sensory input; no distortions from such peculiar human mental processes as emotion or illusion or moral compunction.

The system could handle it. His agglomerated nanoparticle computer, HENRY, could translate the cat's neuron activity and create a composite hologram of the external environment from the cat's eyes, ears, nose, tongue, and paws. Fill in the details from the databank and Chi would be like a phantasm, observing and knowing all.

And so it was, an alien world perceived through the tiny brain and sharp animal senses of Fat Juliet.

She and The Dude eyed their prey. Not the small morsel cheeping on the ground beyond the cedar bush, but the two plump robins scolding them from a lower branch of the oak. One dove at Juliet, then swept back up, well short of her reach. At twenty-two pounds, Juliet conserved her energy—except for the twitching tail—ready to lunge if a bird made the mistake of landing or coming too close.

A few yards away, The Dude feigned disinterest, lolling on the grass, licking one shoulder then the other, all the while watching the mark. A lanky black-and-white ex-tom, he could cover twice the distance in half the time as Juliet, and every muscle was ready. But here came their ostensible mistress, T.J., across the parking lot, back from her run. Juliet stood and stretched, pushing two front paws forward and her posterior in the air.

The robins' squawks increased in tempo, and one made a dive at her. She ignored it, her eyes fixed on T.J.'s spare form.

The Dude offered no more than an impassive glance and settled his chin onto an extended paw now that the stakeout was over.

T.J. crossed the grass from the sidewalk and picked up the waiting Juliet, cradling the cat in her arms.

"Ju-u-lii-et," she crooned. Then she saw the baby bird. "Bad girl! Leave the bird alone!"

Only that interloper Darren called her "Fat Juliet." T.J. uttered her name—most of the time—in long syllables.

T.J. paused, staring at the robin chick, its neck extended, mouth wide, cheeping, flapping bat-like wings that displayed only the faintest down. She glanced up at the robins hopping from limb to limb above them.

"Come on, Dude. You too, Juliet. Back inside." Holding Juliet under one arm, she reached for The Dude. But he scampered away—down the sidewalk. T.J. followed, clutching Juliet's ample body close to her chest.

There had once been a Romeo. He existed now only in the shadowy depths of Juliet's mind, having been flattened next to the curb at T.J.'s old residence, several boyfriends before Darren. After Romeo came The Dude, and later the reclusive Moriarty.

Juliet settled down for the ride. By the time T.J. slipped past the open outside door, The Dude was at the top of the stairs, facing the apartment's closed door as if he expected it to open with the force of his presence.

"Don't worry me about the bird, Juliet," T.J. said, ruffling Juliet's neck as she climbed the stairs. "I had a rough day. Had to go to the prison again, and you know how that is."

Juliet did, indeed. T.J. often told Juliet intriguing stories—about guns, drugs, and a place called Starbucks. And T.J.'s mood always improved after a therapeutic session with Juliet.

The Dude and Moriarty never stopped to listen. Chasing the feather-tipped toy was The Dude's main entertainment, when he wasn't tomcatting about outside—a wasted effort if there ever was one. Moriarty only sneaked up for a scratch and quick rub, then a pass at the food dish and back off to his lair under T.J.'s bed. No, only Juliet listened—and feigned belief in a world far removed from the reality of the apartment and the parking lot with the leafy oak tree at the corner of the building and the maple overhanging their balcony in back.

Chi's note: *Searching for life forms beyond the realm of physical transport, we A'Onians chanced upon this distant planet, which we have studied and documented at length. More recently, the last hundred thousand or so star circuits, we have focused on the planet's more intelligent denizens— "humans" they call themselves—although their intelligence remains problematic. We have never been able to communicate with them; all attempts resulted in the human subject going mad—or being treated by the others as mad—or worse, proclaiming themselves a god or prophet—with the usual results: outbreaks of fanatical religion, ephemeral empires, and megalomaniacal wars.*

With Juliet draped over one arm, T.J. managed to open the apartment door. The Dude scampered inside, headed toward the kitchen and his food dish. Shoving the door closed with a foot, T.J. crossed the living room to the front window and tried to raise the Venetian blinds with one hand. They didn't budge. She plopped Juliet down on the faded white carpet—picked to a rough shag by The Dude—and wrestled the blinds upward at an angle, sending dust motes dancing in the light around her head and shoulders.

The room held little furniture—a scuffed brown sofa, a coffee table buried under stacks of books and magazines, and a CD player on top of a bookcase fashioned from cinder blocks and painted planks. The air was fusty with the smell of old carpet, old furniture, and three cats.

On the wall by the couch was T.J.'s prized possession: a Black Forest clock she'd inherited from her father. The pendulum went click-chic, click-chic, click-chic. Despite the uneven beat, it plodded on, and T.J. wound it each night, sometimes checking twice to ensure it never stopped. On the hour and half-hour, the clock sounded dull, "ka-chuks," since the door was broken and wouldn't open to release the cuckoo. But always the correct number of "ka-chuks."

Juliet at her heels, T.J. strode to the corner and pulled the brass chains down to raise the weights, reaching over the plastic fence she'd installed to foil The Dude's attacks. As she finished, the clock ka-chuked six times, and the little door shuddered under the futile blows of the cuckoo.

In the kitchen, Juliet paused for a few bites from her food dish, one of three in an array of brown pellets on the checkerboard floor, while T.J. retrieved a quart of milk from the refrigerator and a glass from the cabinet. The Dude had already moved on.

"That jerk, the one I told you about," T.J. said. "You know, the murder guy." She poured the milk into the glass and replaced the carton in the refrigerator. "He wants me to argue he wasn't there . . . He has an al-i-bi." A snort of disgust produced a coughing spasm. T.J. wiped her mouth and nose with the bottom of her t-shirt and leaned against the counter.

"I told him I don't believe him, and he-e-e got mad at me. Said I was his lawyer and I had to do what he told me . . . What a mean dude."

A different tone from when she said, "The Dude."

"I don't like him. He's different from the other guys I get. They drop out of school—or maybe get kicked out," she sighed, "and just sort of slip into stuff with their 'homeys.' Then they all go 'round packing heat. My God, Juliet, they're only kids!" She grimaced and shook her head. "A fight and 'bang,' somebody's hurt. Or worse." A deep breath and another sigh.

Juliet rubbed against T.J.'s leg, and T.J. reached down to scratch Juliet's tawny fur and run her hand down Juliet's back.

"They do a little shoplifting, a few petty thefts, some drugs, and before long it's armed robbery. Then off to finishing school at the prison. I feel sorry for them . . . Well, some of 'em . . . and their mothers. Oh shit . . . I don't know, Juliet . . . " She trailed off as she took another swallow of milk, then squatted down next to Juliet. Juliet arched her back for more ministrations to the fur down her spine and tail.

"There are even girls . . . a lot younger than me, having babies that're gonna end up just as bad off as they are, baby mamas making babies . . . Oh God." She finished the milk— and gave another sigh. "Guess that makes me sound like a bigot, huh, Juliet?" She roughly kneaded Juliet's neck, to Juliet's rising pleasure.

T.J. stood and opened the refrigerator. Reaching inside, she added, "But that's the kind of stuff Darren says." She poured herself more milk and restored the carton to its rightful place.

"This dude," she turned away from the fridge and shook her head at Juliet, "he's bad, just plain bad . . . And I know he was there. He calls himself the Hex Man. Well, the prosecutor's gonna hex his butt this time. He has an informant. One of Hex Man's homeys done ratted on him . . . but, my God, I can't tell the Hex Man because they may go and snuff the guy. That prosecutor, Al . . . you know, I told you about him. The jerk. Well, he shouldn't have let it slip; the prick shouldn't have told me . . . Shit!"

Holding the glass of milk in one hand, she drifted out of the kitchen and into the small dining room, stopping beside the table to stare out the sliding glass door. Juliet trotted along behind, then past T.J. to station herself on her haunches near the door. Beyond the glass door, the sun still brightened the leaves on the maple tree and filled most of the balcony.

"I don't know what to do, Juliet. The judge won't let me withdraw just because my client's a friggin jerk . . . He says they're all jerks. Dammit!" This time an emphatic sigh. "I'm his second lawyer, anyhow."

The Dude appeared from drinking his fill at the porcelain pond in the bathroom and growled at his food dish. He looked up at T.J. as if he expected his bedtime tuna already, and it wasn't there.

Oblivious to The Dude's demand, T.J. pulled out a chair from the table and sat down, still staring out the door. Above the table, a gold-and-white Wal-Mart chandelier dangled at an angle, twinkling in the sunlight reflected by a cluster of wine and beer bottles on the balcony.

Juliet jumped up onto a thick blue cushion in the seat of a second chair catty-cornered to T.J.'s. Assuming her sphinx pose, Juliet stared fixedly at her ward as The Dude came over to be scratched. T.J. rubbed her hand along his neck and back. His rasping purrs brought a quick change in T.J.'s musings.

"What am I going to do with you two and that baby robin?"

That blasted Robin again.

"Soon as you go back out there, you'll be after it." T.J. gave The Dude a gentle shake, which he took as the signal to go find the feathered toy for T.J. to throw across the room.

Moriarty was just peering around the corner from the hallway when a knock sounded at the door.

"Hey, babe, you there? Finish your run?" Darren's muffled voice. T.J. rose to answer it, and Moriarty disappeared back into the bedroom.

"Hey babe, yourself. 'Course I'm here." She hurried to the door and opened it. As she did, The Dude whisked past her and between Darren's legs.

Darren reached out to give T.J. a hug. Ignoring him, T.J. strained forward to see where The Dude had gone.

Now that didn't take a genius to see where he was going. Juliet knew The Dude was already out the downstairs door and into the parking lot.

"Oh damn!" T.J. said. "Now he'll go after the birds."

"Ah, don't worry about him," Darren said from the doorway. "Any bird he catches deserves to be caught."

"You don't understand," T.J. said. "There's a baby on the ground, and if the parents try to feed it . . ." She started after The Dude, but Darren's outstretched hand stopped her.

"Huh," he said. "That's how nature works. Survival of the fittest . . . cleans up the gene pool. Something we need more of around here."

Juliet approved of his observation on Mother Nature. Indeed, she usually agreed with Darren. A nice combination, those two, Juliet thought. Maybe if they have kittens, they'll be a lovely black-and-white combo like The Dude.

"Come on, Darren, I had a terrible day." Through the open door, Juliet could see T.J. shake off Darren's hand on her arm. "I gotta go get The Dude before The Dude gets the bird." Their footsteps sounded on the stairs, T.J.'s light and tripping, Darren's heavy and thumping.

Before long, T.J. was back—without The Dude or Darren. Leaving the front door open, she darted into the kitchen and grabbed two oven mitts from a hook above the counter and a shoebox out of the recycling bin in the corner. As the door slammed shut again, Juliet shifted to her other side. Time for a nap. The cuckoo ka-chuked seven times against its broken door.

All too soon, T.J. returned. She carried the shoebox in front of her, and The Dude tagged along behind. Still no Darren.

As T.J. went past the table, the box emitted small cheeping sounds. Juliet sat up.

Doing a little dance to block The Dude, T.J. edged out the sliding glass door and rammed it shut behind her. She gently deposited the box on the floor of the balcony, still partially filled with sunlight. After adjusting the shoebox into a shaded spot, T.J. came back inside, quickly closing the door behind her, and went to the couch for her purse. She rummaged around in it and pulled out her cell phone.

The cheeps beyond the glass intensified.

From her chair, Juliet could see the baby bird sequestered in a nest of dead pine needles and grass, its thin neck stretched up, its beak wide, crying out to the dark interior of the maple tree. On this side of the door sat The Dude, nose to the glass, watching cat TV. The food channel.

The cuckoo clock ka-chuked the half hour.

In the living room, T.J. paced from the window with the crooked blinds, back past the Salvation Army sofa, and into the dining room. She listened and talked and waved one arm in the air, finally stopping to point out at the balcony. Then she said "goodbye" and tossed the phone on the couch next to her purse.

Standing by the door, hands on hips, she informed her audience that she had called Cecile, a good friend who rescued animals, wild and tame. Cecile Juliet loved. A large accommodating lap and the fingers of a true cat masseuse.

"Cecile says I should feed it bits of tuna."

Tuna?

"And Darren is wrong. It's just an old wives' tale that if you touch a baby bird, the parents won't come back to it."

Giving Juliet a passing scratch behind the ears, T.J. went over to the sliding glass door and looked out at the bird. After a moment, she disappeared into the bedroom and returned, holding up a pair of tweezers. Then to the kitchen and the whir of a can opener and back to the sliding glass door. First patiently explaining to The Dude why he couldn't go out, then gently turning him aside several times, she slipped through the door and closed it behind her. She knelt by the box and held out the tweezers toward the chick.

Juliet flicked her tail against the back of the chair. That was *cat* tuna.

The bird lunged at the first bite but after that kept dodging the tweezers.

Juliet's ears went forward in disapproval. Ungrateful wretch.

Finally defeated, T.J. came back inside. Depositing tweezers on the sink and tuna in the refrigerator, she extracted a quart of ice cream from the freezer, then ransacked several drawers to come up with a large serving spoon. She slumped down in the chair beside Juliet's. Lips pursed in thought, she dug out a chunk of ice cream. Caramel crunch.

Juliet preferred vanilla, but she would try a taste if offered. It was.

"Oh, Juliet, what am I going to do? The bird won't eat."

Holding up the empty spoon, T.J. sighed and stared out the sliding glass door. Juliet watched her, and the spoon, with unblinking eyes.

On his haunches at the door, The Dude remained transfixed by the cheeping only a few feet away. Juliet gave one ear a twitch. He's so dumb he thinks that if he sits there long enough, the glass will just go away. When they neutered that tom, they started at the wrong end.

"And Darren left mad," T.J. said. "He thinks I'm silly worrying about the baby robin. I told him he knew me; I couldn't just let a creature die like that . . . He was already mad about Hex Man. He even yelled at me."

She took another bite of ice cream.

"Makes him mad to see me dealing with them . . . trying to keep 'em out of jail." She rapped the spoon on the edge of the container. "I tried to tell him he had advantages they didn't have and that just made him madder. Said I'm one to talk about advantages!" She shook her head and finished the last of the ice cream.

Placing the container on the table, T.J. reached over and ran her hand down Juliet's back. Juliet arched her hindquarters and waved her tail in the air.

T.J. stood and walked to the sliding door and stared out. Then she turned and leaned her back against the glass.

"Darren says . . . first he said he didn't want to tell me . . . that Al has a recording of Hex talking to his girlfriend." Al, the prosecutor. "He's crazy, Darren said . . . and his girlfriend offered to beat it out of me!" She shook her head. "Al shouldn't have told me about the snitch."

She came back and pulled her chair closer to Juliet's.

"Oh, Juliet. I just think Darren's worried about me . . . I'm worried about me. Hex calls me 'that skinny little white girl.'" She took a deep breath. "Oh, God. Maybe I did say something to make him think I know who ratted on him . . . Look! Look, Juliet, there's the mother bird."

A sharp "chik, chik, chik," came from the maple, and a robin hopped from a limb near the balcony onto the railing. With alarmed chirps, it answered the rising, insistent cheeps emanating from the box.

The Dude patted the glass with an outstretched paw.

The robin hopped back and forth on the railing but came no farther. Then it left.

T.J. picked up Juliet and hugged her close. "Maybe it'll come back, Ju-u-li-et. Maybe we can save the baby after all."

Now the chick was up on the edge of the box and cheeping frantically for its parent. It toppled out onto the cement floor near the edge of the balcony.

"Oh my gosh! It's going to fall off!"

T.J. dumped Juliet onto the carpet and rushed to the sliding door. Roughly shoving The Dude aside, she ran out and lifted the baby bird back into the box. The cheeping stopped.

After gently rearranging the chick in its ersatz nest, T.J. retreated through the sliding door, carefully blocking The Dude's exit with her foot. The cheeps quickly resumed, though not as loud. T.J. and the cats watched and waited, Juliet on T.J.'s lap, The Dude by the door. Even Moriarty came all the way into the living room.

After a few long minutes, the robin returned to the railing. A small worm dangled from its beak. The cheeping became frantic, desperate, but this time the baby bird stayed in the box.

The Dude pressed his nose against the glass. His tail twitched and gave a slight shudder.

Not moving from the balcony railing, the robin crooked its head one way, then another. After looking around for only a few seconds, it left—despite its offspring's frantic calls.

They kept their vigil, T.J. stroking Juliet's neck and back and not talking. Twilight seeped into the room, then filled the balcony and shrouded the tree. The clock on the living room wall ka-chuked eight times, and T.J. made another try at feeding the baby chick with the tweezers, with no success.

The Dude and Juliet went down the stairs and outside for their nightly patrol. By the time they returned, The Dude at a run and Juliet at a plodding walk, the inside lights were on. With the finality of night, the cheeps in the box had ceased.

T.J. dumped a heaping spoonful of tuna into each of their dishes and a package of instant ramen noodle soup into a pot on the stove. Before they all settled in for the night—The Dude on the sofa, Moriarty in the box springs under T.J.'s bed, and Juliet curled up on top of the blanket—T.J. wound the cuckoo clock again.

In the first gray light of morning, the cheeping began anew, first intermittent, then incessant and urgent. T.J. rose at the sound and joined by The Dude and Juliet, watched for the sun to yellow the east side of the maple—and for the mother or father bird to return. Neither did.

Before she left for work, T.J. once more presented the chick with a dollop of tuna in the tweezers. No luck.

She waited to the last minute to leave. From her rushing about, Juliet could tell she was late. By the time she crossed the living room to the front door, the cuckoo had ka-chuked against its door nine times, and the cheeps coming from the balcony were fainter and farther apart.

All morning, The Dude remained glued to cat TV, watching for the return of his prey and leaving only for a few routine patrols around the apartment. Juliet perched on her chair and snoozed, occasionally venturing away to lower the level in her food dish and raise the level in the litter box. Moriarty circled by Juliet's chair a few times but showed no interest in the greater world beyond his transit.

The pendulum on the cuckoo clock swung back and forth, click-chic, click-chic, click-chic. Each hour and half-hour, the cloistered cuckoo struck the closed door, faithfully advancing the day.

As the midday sun filled the balcony—and the shoebox— the cheeps outside faded, then stopped. Finally, at five ka-chuks of the cuckoo clock, The Dude awoke from his forgotten vigil and migrated to the front door to await T.J.'s return. Moriarty took a few desultory swipes at him, received a blow across the nose, and settled down a few feet away. From the blue cushion above them, Juliet maintained her feline decorum and gazed placidly at the inanimate objects in the living room. The Salvation Army sofa, the cluttered coffee table, the broken Venetian blinds.

T.J. did not come. The cuckoo clock ka-chuked six, and the evening sun slanted into the maple and yellowed the front of the balcony and the railing. There was a low rumble of thunder, and shortly after, the sun winked out. It grew dark, and a pattering of drops beat a cadence just beyond the silent box on the balcony.

Juliet and the others waited, the cuckoo made repeated attempts to break through its shuttered exit, and T.J. still did not come. Juliet settled down in her chair, her eyes open wide now, watching the front door and The Dude on the floor in front of it. At the sound of thunder, Moriarty fled to the box springs. The food dishes were empty. Even the scattering of pellets was gone, vacuumed up by The Dude.

The cuckoo clock gave a few labored ka-chuks, the pendulum went click-chic, chic, . . . chic, . . . chic, and then it stopped as the weights settled to rest, tilted against each other like drunken sailors, on the carpeted floor.

This has not gone well at all, Chi decided. According to HENRY's calculations of the probabilities, T.J. was probably waylaid on her way home by Hex Man's girlfriend. Perhaps HENRY could change a factor or two, a minor adjustment somewhere back in time, and deflect the young woman from an intersecting trajectory with her nemesis.

All he had to work with was the cat. Some action by the fat Juliet that would change what T.J. was doing, her story arc. He adjusted the program, giving new instructions to HENRY, and they linked once again with the neurons in Juliet's brain— at the same point where they had started before.

Fat Juliet and The Dude eyed their prey. Not the small morsel cheeping on the ground just beyond the cedar bush, but the plump robins scolding them from a lower branch of the young oak.

Chi made a short jump—until Darren arrived. Perhaps here was the moment to alter the course of events, like the proverbial beat of the butterfly wing. But how to use the cat? Fat Juliet's senses and normal reactions. A neuron prompted here and there—

"Hey, babe, you there?   Finish your run?" Darren's muffled voice.

"Hey babe, yourself. . . . 'Course I'm here."

T.J. hurried to the door and opened it. As soon as she did, The Dude whisked past her and between Darren's legs.

Chi moved the time cursor forward again, waiting for the right moment to trigger the right combination of neurons in the fat cat's brain.

T.J. started down the stairs after The Dude, but Darren's outstretched hand stopped her.

"That's the way nature works. Survival of the fittest . . . cleans up the gene pool. Something we need more of around here."

Juliet was considering the wisdom of Darren's observation when she sat up on the cushion, gave two hacking coughs, and launched a hairball onto the floor, along with some yellowish liquid that landed on the seat of T.J.'s chair.

"Oh, damn!" T.J. said, turning to give Juliet a reproving glare. "I've had a terrible day, and Juliet just made a mess. And the chair! Now I've got to clean it up."

As they came inside, T.J. related to Darren what she had told Juliet—who settled back on her cushion and watched as T.J. retrieved paper towels and a wet rag from the kitchen and began the usual hairball ritual. While cleaning the floor and chair, T.J. continued her story. Darren listened more expressively than Juliet had and became more and more agitated.

"Look, T.J., just get out of the damn case. You know how I feel about these people. I have to put up with their crap all day. All night sometimes." Darren had a silver badge and a gun in a holster on his belt.

"I can't do that, Darren. He's still my client." T.J. sat down across from Darren, who was staring silently at T.J. The cuckoo ka-chuked seven times against its broken door.

"Even if I don't like him," T.J. said, "I have to give him the best representation the state can buy." She laughed. "Which ain't much good at all based on what I know."

"Right! I didn't want to tell you this, but Al has a recording of your man talking to his girlfriend." Al, the prosecutor, that other jerk T.J. had mentioned. "Those dopes don't even stop to think that their phone calls are monitored, even when they're staring at a row of bars. They just pop off—"

"Okay, okay. So what did he say?"

"Well, your Hex man was complaining how you don't believe him. He thinks . . . no, he knows . . . you know something you haven't told him. He's crazy, T.J. His girlfriend offered to beat it out of you—to put it politely."

T.J. looked startled and gave a low squeak like the mouse Juliet had happened on outside the laundry room.

"Beat it out of me!"

"Hex isn't just another poor street kid. He's rock-hard mean. And I know the girlfriend. She's bad—and she's into all this martial arts crap. She beat the . . . Oh, I don't mean to scare you. But damn it all, you need to stop taking on those guys as clients. Just turn 'em down—"

"How am I gonna get trial experience? . . . Besides, I told Judge Larkins I'd take appointed cases. I don't get a choice of which ones." She made a disgusted face at Darren. "Like I can say: 'that looks like a winner, so I'll take it, but I don't want any thugs, liars, or all-around creeps.'"

"Aw, T.J., you know what I mean." Darren reached across the corner of the table and took her hand. "You don't even like this stuff. You told me all you wanted was to open a bookstore."

T.J. was quiet for a few seconds, then pulled her hand away. She stood and walked to the sliding door. She stared out onto the balcony. Then she turned and, after glancing at Juliet, started toward the front door.

"I gotta get The Dude before The Dude gets the bird," she said, her lips tight.

"Oh, shit . . ." Darren started, but she was already on her way out.

Darren followed. On his way past Juliet's chair, he gave her a quick scratch, then a sharp tug on her tail. Claws extended, Juliet's front paw lashed out at his hand—a fraction of an inch short. Close enough to let him know who was boss.

As Darren shut the door, Juliet settled back down and closed her eyes.

Before long, T.J. was back—without The Dude or Darren. Leaving the front door open, she darted into the kitchen and grabbed two oven mitts . . .

Chi shifted away from HENRY'S four-dimensional display. This was all too familiar. Darren had left just as before, and now T.J. was following the same course as before. Little if any variation from her trajectory to—Chi didn't know what had happened last time since he was following this little drama through the brain of a house cat who never ventured far from the comfort of her cushion or T.J.'s bed. And HENRY had only a well-calculated guess.

Chi decided to let things run their course for a while. And consider what he could do to alter the result.

The chick was up on the edge of the box and cheeping frantically for its parent. It toppled out and onto the cement floor.

"Oh my gosh! It's going to fall off the balcony!"

T.J. dumped Juliet onto the carpet and rushed to the sliding door.

Chi waved his hand across HENRY'S time-dimension control. A little further. Are these humans governed exclusively by fate? Predestined to follow the same vector and end up the same no matter what?

They kept their vigil, T.J. stroking Juliet's neck and back and not talking while darkness seeped into the room, filled the balcony, and shrouded the maple tree. T.J. made two more tries to feed the baby chick, again with no success. As the cuckoo clock ka-chuked a single time, T.J. released The Dude and Juliet on their nightly prowl. They returned at T.J.'s call for tuna. Then to bed, The Dude on the sofa, Moriarty in the box springs, and Juliet curled up on top of the blanket next to T.J.

Chi pondered. Still no significant diversion in T.J.'s course. He couldn't just let her plunge forward as she was doing. But all he had was Juliet. Who never did anything outside the usual cat behavior, including responding to T.J.'s attentions. And T.J. to her.

And T.J. to her? Perhaps there was something there for the morning.

In the first gray light, the cheeps began anew, first intermittent, then incessant and urgent. At the rising cry, T.J. rose from the bed and—joined by The Dude and Juliet— stood at the sliding glass door to watch the sun yellow the east side of the maple. But there was no sign of the chick's parents.

Before she left for work, T.J. again presented the chick with a dollop of tuna in the tweezers. Again, no luck.

Juliet felt queasy seeing all that good tuna going to waste. She jumped off her cushion and went to eat a few bites from her dish. Then she drank some water and headed for the litter box. At the edge of the hall carpet, well short of the litter, the urge to pee hit her like the business end of a broom. She froze and made a puddle on the floor. Then she puked on the carpet.

"Oh, shit!" T.J., on her way out the door, dropped her briefcase and came back to survey the damage.

Juliet circled the small pond she had created and the yellow glop of food, examining them. Puzzled. What's going on here?

"Are you ill, Juliet?" T.J. said, squatting down beside her and gently rubbing the fur at Juliet's neck. "Do we need to go to the Vet? You have another urinary tract infection?"

Juliet looked up and gave a pitiful meow. She hated the Vet. But she really didn't feel well.

T.J. shook her head. "I can't take you now . . . can't miss docket call," she muttered as she scratched behind Juliet's ear. "And today's Ezee's plea. He's just sixteen, you see, Juliet, and his only defense is he shot the tires, and his bro shot the driver. We need this judge . . ." Standing, she raised her voice. "I'll come back after lunch and check on you. Okay, girl?"

T.J. deposited Juliet back on her cushion, then cleaned up the mess and sprayed an odor suppressant on the edge of the carpet. Then she closed the bedroom door, blocking Juliet from retreating to T.J.'s unmade bed.

Not long after T.J. left, the cuckoo ka-chuked once for the half hour. And after that ten ka-chuks on the hour.

While The Dude remained fixated by cat TV, Juliet snoozed on her chair. After more ka-chuks, she felt much better and ventured off to visit her food dish and the litter box. No more accidents.

As the midday sun filled the balcony, the cheeps faded, then stopped. By the time the cuckoo gave twelve ka-chuks, The Dude had relocated to the couch.

At half past one, a key sounded in the lock.

Juliet popped up from her torpor and The Dude jumped from the couch. After a quick stretch, he headed to the door. The muscles in his hindquarters rippled as he prepared to bolt as soon as it opened.

From beyond the door, farther down the stairs, came a voice, gravelly and harsh.

"Yo, girl! I need to talk *to you*."

Juliet cocked her head to one side. That tone did not bode well for polite conversation.

The Dude retreated and settled back on his haunches in the foyer. Moriarty, who had been lying in the sunlight by the window, split for the bedroom. His retreat foiled, he scratched at the closed bedroom door.

The front door opened a crack, and Juliet could see a narrow sliver of white legs, a gray suit, and brown hair.

"Wh . . . what do you want?" T.J.'s voice.

"You have some scoop my man needs—to get his life back together."

The voice came closer, and a dusky hand displaying an array of gold rings with large stones—green, white, blue, red—gripped the doorframe just above T.J.'s head.

"Somebody's ratted on him, and we need to talk to the little snitch."

"There's nothing I can tell you," T.J. said. The door tremored slightly but didn't open any farther. "You're Hex Man's girlfriend, aren't you? He . . . you . . . go tampering with witnesses . . . you'll be . . . you'll both be in big trouble . . . bigger than he's in now."

"Aw, ain't nobody gonna hurt the guy." A long muscular leg in calf-length black spandex pants and a sparkling gold high-heel shoe appeared at the bottom of the door.

"Hex's in the cage, girl, so's he can't do nuthin, no how. We just wanta help the little rat get outta this mess he's got hisself into . . . Maybe he'd like to, you know, take a little vacation." A deep chuckle came from beyond T.J.'s shoulder. "You know, Jamaica or someplace nice like that." Now the voice of reason. "We understand how it is when the heat starts promisin' stuff and all. He just needs to remember who his friends and brothers are . . . who's gonna look after him . . . Ain't the cops, that's for damn sure."

"Look . . . go tell Hex he needs to leave this alone."

"Naw, ain't nobody gonna tell the Hex Man nuthin . . . Now, come on, out with it, lawyer girl, and everybody'll be happy . . . Peace in the valley, joy in the house."

In the opening, a dark face with bright red lips and iridescent blue eye shadow, a high forehead pulled back by tight cornrows, came close to T.J.'s face. The hand with the rings slid farther inside and grabbed the inner doorjamb, the rings pressed tightly against it.

Juliet watched, feeling more than a little anxious at T.J.'s plight and willing T.J. to do something. She did. First pushing the door inward, T.J. jerked it shut on the exposed hand and ringed fingers on the door jamb.

Hex's girlfriend screamed, then yelled, "Ow, ow, shit . . . you bitch!" The hand and ominous face disappeared as T.J. shoved the door open again and jumped inside the apartment. But not quick enough.

"Goddamn you! I'll fix you!" Using her undamaged hand, the woman clutched at T.J.'s arm and yanked her back through the doorway.

Now it was up to Juliet. She popped up on the cushion, to her highest arched height, hair bristling on her neck, and gave a piercing howl usually reserved for the mangy alley cat out back.

With this signal and the door wide open, The Dude launched himself through the tangle of feet, sending the last and biggest obstacle in his path stumbling backward in a frantic two-step. A high-heel-clad foot came down on The Dude's hind paw. He screeched. Whirling about, he sank his teeth into an exposed ankle just above the gold shoe. Then he raked his claws down the woman's bare leg from spandex to shoe, throwing her off balance and eliciting another shriek of pain.

"Oh, fuck! Fuck this shit! Get off me, you goddamn cat! Get off!"

Frantically trying to shake the wild animal off her leg, the woman released her grip, and T.J. fell backward into the room and down to one knee. The Dude briefly pressed his attack and then, with a last, long, angry yowl, shot down the stairs—aided by a glancing assist from a pointed gold toe.

By now, T.J. was on her feet. She slammed the door shut.

Though free of the devil cat, the woman continued yelling in pain. "What'd you let that fucking animal do to me? . . . Shit! Shit! Shit! Look at the fucking blood! Goddamn you, you skinny white bitch, I'm gonna get blood poisonin' from that dumb-ass cat!"

The woman started rattling the doorknob and pounding on the door panel, but T.J. had set the lock and thrown the bolt. The door shuddered from the blows.

Fumbling in her purse, T.J. pulled out a cell phone and tapped furiously at it while shrinking back into the dining room. She stumbled against the table, grabbed at the edge, and missed. Scrambling backward to avoid falling, she dropped the cell phone as she bounced off the sliding glass door.

T.J. jerked her head around to stare out at the balcony. Juliet followed the stare. Could she escape that way? Climb over the railing?

The front door shook under pounding fists and vicious kicks accompanied by more screams of rage. And finally, a full-body rush. At this time of day, nobody would be in the downstairs apartment to hear the ruckus.

T.J. turned frightened eyes back to the entrance as another body blow fell on the door. And another, and another. The doorjamb gave and splintered in a loud crack, pulling the lock loose in the middle so that the only thing holding the door closed was the dead bolt at the top.

Exerting herself for a second time in the same day, Juliet stood on her toes and arched her back and tail. She hissed and, starting from a low rumbling growl, emitted a rising, blood-curdling screech designed to strike terror in any living being who could hear. Especially one who had already felt The Dude's fury.

The front door stopped shaking under the woman's blows. For good measure, Juliet let out a second screech. Time to press the attack.

Loud voices came from outside, and seconds later, the sound of clicking heels retreating down the stairs. Then a knock. Satisfied with her victory, Juliet settled back onto her cushion.

"Babe, you okay?" Darren. Well, maybe he had helped some.

"She's gone." Another knock, louder this time. "You okay? . . . Let me in, T.J. She won't mess with you now, and I'll deal with her later."

T.J. opened the door and Darren put his arms around her. She started sobbing against his white shirt.

"Hex Man, right?" Darren held her with one arm and stroked her hair with his free hand.

"Why would he do that? Why? How could he be so stupid?" A sob. "I'm trying to help him."

"You can't help him. Not the way he wants. This is how it is on the street, T.J. You can't change it."

She took several deep breaths and stopped crying as quickly as she had begun. "Yeah, I guess," she said into his shirt.

Breaking free of him, she wiped first one cheek and then the other with the back of her hand. She looked around, then came to Juliet's chair and picked up the big tabby in both arms, hugging her tightly. Darren watched her in silence.

Walking to the sliding glass door, T.J. stared out at the sun slanting into the maple and lighting the front part of the balcony and the railing. Absentmindedly, she scratched Juliet's head and looked at the tree and the small shoebox in front of the door.

"Darren, would you do me a favor?"

"Sure, babe. What is it?"

"Will you bury the baby robin for me?"

The End, according to Chi

TIME TO GO

Pausing, he places his hand on the bar to open the door and watches through the glass. Bodies circulate in the open area around the high reception desk, some with purpose, some with none. The almost-but-not-quite abandoned and forgotten.

Near the desk are two blanket-swathed, wispy-white-haired androgynous figures in wheelchairs, head down, chin on chest, sleeping, dying. Opposite them, guarding the hallway from an old-fashioned straight-back chair, is an aristocratically gray-haired man, blue-and-white plaid shirt pressed against slat ribs and chest, erect back pressed against the chair back, oxygen bottle on wheels by his side. Eyes stare at a distant horizon: a bucolic scene of green fields and green trees? Blue mountains and rose-hued sunset? In the nose and mouth, the scent and taste of clean, crisp air?

Clear tubes run oxygen into the nostrils. The nares flare—in, out; in, out. A rasping wheeze rises in the throat, drawing on a wellspring of rot deep within, followed by a gurgling, strangled cough that becomes a crescendo, resonant, stentorian, filling the entrance as the visitor opens the door and enters.

Beyond the man, down the hall, she sits by herself in a wheelchair, detached from the others, waiting for him to come through the glass doors. Watching, small steady eyes alert in a pasty face. Even as he opens the door, she is moving, pulling the wheelchair forward with her feet between the footrests, pushing at the wheels with warped, arthritic hands, her hips and knees refusing any longer to support her burgeoning weight. Her torn red bedroom slippers, in which she no longer treads, go "whisp-whisp" on the linoleum floor as they slide back and forth. Whisp-whisp, back and forth. Deep wrinkled face, now creased with a wide smile; crow's-feet stretching out from her eyes, from the sunken corners of her mouth. Blue-tinted hair, newly permed by the in-house beautician just for him. On the left side of the white-white forehead, just below the blue-white hair, is an angry red sore the size of a nickel.

Today they will go riding—through the town and out into the rolling countryside to look at the red, yellow, and purple colors of fall. Where they go doesn't matter to her at all. Just so they go, as they did the day before and the day before that.

Except, sometimes, they meander through the cemetery, down narrow lanes between row upon row of graves, until they reach the plot where his father lies, dead these forty years. On the granite monument that cost more than they, the widow and sons, could then afford, "Whither thou goest, I will go," her name and date of birth engraved next to his. Never another man for her, she would say with a toss of her head. Hang up the phone when some old goat called and asked her out to dinner. Better the nights alone with a hammer under the bed.

She can't get out of the car now—feel the grass under her feet and touch the stone, gaze at names and dates—and doesn't want to anymore. She'll be back here soon enough, to stay, she says. But she'll tell him again that the gravestone's "plumb filthy"—aging granite, covered with lichen and soot—"you come over here, son, and clean it up." And he never does.

On Christmas and Easter, he takes her to buy artificial flowers—plastic roses and lilies—and places them in the monument's granite vases, where they will remain, un-removed, and fade and sag through spring and summer and fall. But the azalea she planted some twenty years past blooms every year, brilliant red next to the darkening stone, just as the white flowers on the dogwood's gnarled limbs above it turn to green.

After the cemetery, they'll go through the town, where their memories are buried, go past empty store fronts and vacant lots, the new pool hall and the old church, now for sale. The decaying neighborhood, the house his father built, now home to strangers, a small family like theirs, only different—different lives, different cares, different joys. Different race, different opportunities.

She will count traffic lights, raising a bent finger, "One, two, three, four," counting each set at each intersection. Gleeful when they reach five-points, a double light on each of five intersecting streets, and she counts to ten.

No questions on family, so he repeats the same news every circuit: what the granddaughter is doing, where the grandson is living now. Where he was before he arrived on Friday. He asks how his aunts are holding up with age, two older than she, how his cousins are. She makes no comments on events in a world in which she no longer lives and has no interest in. It's all irrelevant to her. Has been for years. All she watches on the small TV in her room are game shows, Wheel of Fortune and Vanna White, and black-and-white reruns, Rockford Files, Lucy, and Andy and Barney Fife, same as they watched while eating TV dinners on metal trays in front of the first television set she bought after his father died. A television that his father had always refused to buy.

From behind her (as she moves, whisp, whisp, whisp, down the hall) comes the same cry as last night and the night before: "He'p me! He'p me! Somebody he'p me!"

None of the white-uniformed nurses or blue-clad attendants move to go to the room at the back, from which the cry echoes again. "He'p me! He'p me! Somebody, please he'p me! He'p me, he'p me!" Over and over and over.

A swathed mummy in one of the wheelchairs reaches out a hand to grab his arm and mumbles noises that may have been words. He slips past the hand and starts down the hall. From the floors and walls and the doorways he passes come a palimpsest of odors—industrial cleaner, disinfectant, antiseptic wash, and underlying them all the stench of urine, old and new.

Down the hall, a blank-faced wraith in a gray housedress glides out an open doorway and moves in behind the wheelchair, makes as if to push it along. She manages only to grasp air, then pantomimes propelling the chair onward, across the checkerboard tiles toward him.

Whisp, whisp, go the slippers on the floor.

She's too heavy for him to lift now. His own shoulders and knees and lungs don't work the way they should. His breath is short when he climbs the stairs and his heart races when he wakes in the dark hours of the morning. He drinks too much. Works too hard.

Now it takes both him and an attendant to hoist and pivot her bulk from the wheelchair into the passenger's seat of the rented car while she clutches the top of the door. This woman who single-handedly hauled mattresses and bedsprings outside to air in the April sun, who cleaned and cooked and washed every day, year after year after year until they were gone, husband and sons. Carried baskets of clothes down steep basement steps and, once the clothes were washed and through the Maytag wringer, lugged them—galvanized metal washtub bouncing on her thighs, outside into the yard. Hung the wet clothes in the sun with wooden clothespins on wire clotheslines strung between metal poles shaped like crosses. Carried him to doctors when he was six years old and couldn't walk, and she had to because they owned no car.

Will he, like her, be here someday? Or is the alternative better?

The money's gone. The last bit of it went for her coffin and the prepaid funeral. He didn't get the vault to keep the coffin and its contents dry. He follows logic. The flesh dissolves; even bones and hair disintegrate over time, over eons, whatever human efforts to preserve it. Even the pharaohs. At most withered mummies—or fossils. And then nothing but cosmic dust.

The resurrection of the body a myth, a joke played by humorless ecclesiastics. Dust-to-dust, that he can believe. Atoms to atoms. And the money saved will buy her one more month in a private room, a mendicant's cell of her own— since she can't tolerate anyone else in her space. Some stranger turning the lights off when she wants them on. Talking when she wants quiet. Changing the channel, hogging the bathroom, leaving the door to the room open.

She may be wrong, his brother says, but she's never in doubt.

For lunch, they will go to a place that mimics a country store, with fried chicken and fried okra and corn bread and sweetened iced tea, and coconut crème pie. Or eggs and grits and ham and red-eye gravy three meals a day. All around them, buttocks spilling over chair seats, bellies resting on tables, jowls puffed out like pumpkins. She will fiddle with the children's game, moving pegs back and forth; drop biscuit crumbs down her chin, grits on the front of her blouse. The top button is still missing, replaced by a safety pin. Refuses to wear the new clothes he buys, prefers her old, even in disrepair.

This finicky woman who never went to town or church without a bath and powders, always immaculately dressed and coiffured, nary wrinkle or spot on her clothes. A scarf at the throat, an unpretentious half-moon hat on her head. A gold-painted dolphin brooch on her blouse. No safety pins then.

Once again, he will tell her not to stuff her mouth full—eggs, grits, and biscuits—roles reversed after three score years of her telling him not to eat so fast. Finished, she will remove her dentures and clean them with a napkin, not-too-discretely in front of heavy breasts, while he grimaces and looks away.

Before, years before, in the old house his father built of concrete blocks and stucco, they would sit at the kitchen table, yellow linoleum top and chrome metal legs, now long relegated to the city dump—it along with the tattered gray carpets, torn curtains, rusty tools, and worn chairs—and laugh, over greasy plates of drive-through food, laugh at some unforgotten adventure when she was young: flying on a dare in an open biplane with a barnstorming pilot; chucking her coat out the shirt mill's second-floor window to sneak out for a matinee, Clark Gable and Carole Lombard in black and white; standing up his father for a boy with a car and he didn't ask her out again for a year, and then only if she promised to be there. And she always kept her promises.

Or some more recent foible. Back then when she lived alone and they laughed at the yellow linoleum kitchen table. Peripatetic searches for quarters and dimes in pay phones and vending machines. The box of fried pies in the freezer when the doctor told her to eat more fruit. The hunt for snuff at the new, organic grocery. The on-going feud with the old man next door. The key ring from the five-and-dime—"If you don't like my driving, stay off the sidewalk."

There had always been something sweet to share: ice cream or a supermarket cake he'd deem unfit to eat. More often, though, a banana pudding still warm on the stove. Her long decline signaled by black-tip meringue, and just before the nadir, before her fall, the scorched filling. Almost, but not quite, inedible, but special, made from a recipe on the wafer box, just for him.

After the fall, came this place: a prison-cell-size room and a single bed against the wall, the blaring television and wailing down the hall, the nostril-haunting smells, the indifferent staff to a ringing bell. No escape, no exit, *huis clos*. It wasn't just that she couldn't drive herself anymore, escape in her car as she had before. At first, a walker, then another fall, and a wheelchair now. Never to rise and walk again. All the Lord could manage, she'd say with a chuckle, was to lift her spirits when he—not the Lord—came to visit.

The list of medicines grows longer and longer. Half psychotropic, half for who knows what. Force the mindless minders and doctors to end one and they add another. Old friends are dead or tucked away by families somewhere else. Visitors are few, only the pastor and ladies from church and a niece or two looking for their long-dead parents in her face, her voice.

No inheritance here, the house sold, the savings depleted; there never were any heirlooms or silver or crystal or Louis Quinze chairs, only pictures and memories and dust. All that remains to pay the bills are Social Security and Medicaid and him.

This woman—uneducated daughter of sharecroppers, widow of a good man who swept floors and cleaned toilets and polished spittoons—was ever proud and willful, not seeking charity from anyone and refusing it if ever offered. Even when his father died and he was fifteen and his brother long gone. After twenty years she went back to work at the same old shirt mill where she had worked before she married, where she had started when she was fourteen.

They always paid their own way, whatever came.

"If we was poor when I was growin' up, we never knowed it," she would say. "And we was never poor in the things that mattered." Had she heard that somewhere, on TV, in small talk with relatives or friends?

But she meant it, every word.

He remembers. After his father died and she finally learned to drive, long rides on the new interstate and KFC chicken in rest stops as the sun set over undulating lanes that would someday take him west, over the distant blue mountains. The breakfasts she left in the oven, dried scrambled eggs and toast, before she went off to work in the dark. The clothes always washed and ironed and folded. The dwindling congregation in the old church where, confident of heaven, she made a ten-dollar deposit every week, not quite a widow's mite, from minimum wages and no benefits at the mill. Sunday dinners spread abundantly and blessed with brevity on their one tablecloth, white with faded red strawberries.

Whisp, whisp, go the slippers on the floor.

And stop.

From her arms, the flesh hangs wrinkled and loose. Ninety years of joys and sorrows are etched in her face. Behind her sunken grin lie pink bare gums, save one lone tooth. Her dentures are out, back in her room in a plastic cup or tucked in her pocket, wrapped in Kleenex.

He leans down to hug her. Her gnarled hands reach out and talon fingers grab his arms, pulling him closer to her.

As they touch, odors waft up to greet him: baby powders, Menthol, and urine. Other smells lurk in the back of his mind: sun-dried towels and sheets, chicken frying, cold cream, red roses on Mother's Day, Evening in Paris perfume.

He presses his smooth-shaved face against the soft dried-apple wrinkles, saying, "You're looking good, Mother." Smiling down at her. "Ready to go?" And thinking, "It's time to go, Mother. It's really time to go."

She pulls his head and ear next to her mouth and hisses past the remaining tooth, "Git me outta here, son. There's too many old people in this place." She shakes his arm. "I can't stand it no more. Ya hear me . . . Git me outta here."

End

BREAK THE BUBBLE

Someday Daniel would have a bubble like theirs: the Chief, across the conference table from him, her assistant to her left, and the Company's head lawyer, a small, rotund bald man, to her right. All of them had bubbles. The assistant, he was sure, had one because she was always there, always ready for any emergency.

"A bubble is not a right," saith the Chief, "bubbles are earned."

Daniel waited, watching, while the Chief, her back to him, talked on a Handy and the head lawyer flipped through the pages of Daniel's report. The assistant, Julia, appeared to be skimming through her e-messages, answering one here and there with quick taps of a long, implanted fingernail specially designed and programmed for the e-phone.

Julia looked up and smiled at Daniel, and he smiled back. Hers was a thoughtful smile, appraising. His was fake.

He had seen her only twice before, once down a hallway and, later, behind the Speaker's dais when the Chief gave one of her pep talks to the assembled workers. Workers who were drones, not much different from Daniel. All of them without personal bubbles.

In the Speaker's Hall, a "bubble for the masses" covered everyone, as it did here in the conference room. But it was a minimal bubble, one that gave only partial protection, just adequate to preserve the workforce.

For a bubble of your own, out in the world, that was another matter. You had to be able to pay for it. Have enough credits.

After this job, Daniel thought, I'll be on track to earn my own bubble. Maybe six months. And one for Rachel.

But it was too late for Rachel. Way too late.

The assistant, Julia, was looking down at her e-messages again or her FacePage fans—or whatever she used to pretend she was doing something useful. Her smile had only lasted a few seconds.

Why the Chief and her lawyer wanted a paper version of his report and only one original was no mystery to Daniel. E-copies were subject to hacking or remote sensing devices, regardless of the type of media or the encryption. But a paper version, typed on an antique IBM Selectric, was absolutely secure, the most secure medium available for someone in his business.

It was secure as long as the paper version didn't get "misplaced" and so long as the person banging the keys was absolutely trustworthy. Someone like Daniel, an on-the-ground researcher with a good pedigree and a sterling track record.

But he wasn't trustworthy. Not after Rachel contracted Callistis-TC1a.

The Chief said "off" in an audible voice and placed her e-phone on the conference table. She stared at Daniel with ice-blue eyes, a Teutonic goddess with short blond hair and ivory skin.

"Now, Mr. Greene," a voice like fingernails scraping on an antique chalkboard, "tell us about Africa." Smarter she was, so it was said, than all the other mavens among the One Hundred. "Tell us how your report can help resolve our troubles."

The troubles in Nigeria: over two billion people packed together in cities across western Africa from the Sahara to the Namib, an area holding some of the most valuable and essential resources left on earth. An average lifespan of fewer than thirty years, half the people sick and dying, and only one percent able to afford bubbles. A cauldron of perpetual revolt, mayhem, and death, even for those in bubbles, premature death when the rebels got past the Guardians. Guardians like Julia. Who would eliminate any threat in an instant, only dust and vapor left of a once-living being.

"Your report gives us, I see," said the head lawyer in a sing-song voice, "full details on the most infected populations. Where they are concentrated," he turned toward the Chief, "and especially where the rebels are operating."

That was the first reason for Daniel's investigation, which he had done mostly by analyzing close-earth satellite images and reviewing communication feeds or extracting data from field reports filed by the Free-World Legion commanders in Africa. Free-World, an ironic mocking of reality, like in some twentieth-century novel.

The Company needed the resources—metals, diamonds, uranium, rare earths—to supply the web of production that drove the Free World from the Elbe to the Straits of Magellan. From Tokyo to Sydney, from Air-cars to Enviro-houses. Most importantly, raw materials for growing personal bubbles impregnable to microbes, viruses, and newbies—unlike the minimal bubbles that could protect spaces no larger than an Enviro-house or a Speaker's Hall or this conference room.

Bubbles were essential for their survival. Now that more and more viruses and bacteria and newbies were resistant to all forms of known medications and mutating faster than new biomedicines could be developed, mutating faster than the smart vaccines and super biologics designed to analyze, adapt, and attack any threat to the human life. The newbies were the smartest living thing, if you could call them living, on earth and in the solar system. The ultimate evolutionary success, the marvel of the known universe.

"Newbies" were a virus-like quasi-protein that had come back to earth with the first manned mission to Callisto, Jupiter's second largest moon. How it had occurred was still not understood, whether on the ship or in the humans who explored the surface. Or how the newbies had coopted thousands of species of existing viruses to become stronger, more resilient, and persistent. The newbies had survived decontamination and almost immediately spread to humans, killing an entire space city within weeks. Isolation stopped the spread for more than a year, then came "the great contagion." Some suspected a Red Mandarin or Caliphate plot, but the Reds and Quaedists had suffered as much as every other fiefdom and city-state around the globe, including those in the Free World.

In response to intensive eradication efforts, and perhaps to preserve the human hosts and not wipe them out completely, the newbies had evolved. Rachel's Callistis-TC1a was only one deadly virulent strain among thousands. Not killing immediately, the newbies allowed their hosts to live long enough for them, the newbies, to replicate and spread more efficiently. They were joined by a score of antibiotic-resistant earth bacteria and viruses that benefited from accelerating mutations, mutations prompted by the mega-doses of drugs used, ineffectively, against the newbies.

Be fruitful and multiply, saith the Lord of hosts. And then die—every human died young.

Until the Company developed the bubble.

The small-space bubble—supplemented with a secure food/water supply chain repeatedly bombarded with radiation—had slowed the spread of the contagion. But there was no way to irradiate humans the same as food and water. Not safely.

A small biologic firm had invented "the personal bubble." It fit an individual like a glove (or as one researcher put it, like one of the condoms from the fourth world), unseen and permanently in place with its own safe irradiation system based on a nano-energy pack no larger than a big toenail. The original bubbles were perfected, patented, and produced by Orange Enterprise, now part of a conglomerate of former energy, biotech, and health companies. The Orange Company.

The head lawyer was going through the report, explaining it to the Chief and occasionally asking Daniel for affirmation or a few words of clarification. Daniel studied them, the head lawyer and the Chief, wondered what it would be like to always live inside a bubble.

Bubbles were invisible to the naked eye—unless the periphery was caught by a sudden change in lighting, like the halo of an earth eclipse on the moon. You had to watch closely and know what to look for.

Daniel knew what to look for.

He had noticed a slight blip, smaller than a shuttle oxygen mask, over the head lawyer's nose and mouth. A nano-tech filtering system for the air the wearer breathed.

Providing security at a charity ball for the sick billions in Africa, he'd seen the same blip on the Chief when a strobe light limned her face and painted a small rainbow on one ivory cheek.

How it worked, he didn't know. Some sort of membrane or magnetic field was involved, so he'd heard. He sought out a nano-bio engineer with whom he had done research in university and occasionally gone slumming in Baja. Asked him if it were possible to make your own bubble. A bubble for Rachel. Before . . .

The engineer only shook his head, said it would be like trying to build your own shuttle to go to Saturn's moons, the opposite extreme of the nanotechnology used for bubbles but the same difficulty—and cost. And, the engineer had whispered, "the bubble is a living thing. Like a second skin, thinner than the meninges over the brain." The engineer had to be careful and whisper low inside a noise field because the Censors were always listening.

Bubbles grew from stem cells, enveloping their owners, and could merge temporarily with another bubble for intimacy, if the parties wished. Or for protection. That was another one of Julia's functions, a second bubble always there to protect the Chief.

But bubbles were not foolproof. The irradiation, constantly applied over many years, led to cell mutations and aggressive cancers, especially of the skin and body cavities. Most of these maladies were treatable now, but the body remained weakened afterward. So even the bubble people succumbed to some disease or accelerated aging by fifty years on average.

Very few people could afford a personal bubble at a million F-W bucks, though that was much less than the cost of the earlier ones. Maybe five percent of the Free World's population could, even less of the second and third worlds', and a mere fraction of the fourth in South Asia. Almost everyone else was ill by twenty-five and dead by thirty.

Like Rachel, dying now, and only twenty-six.

How had Daniel survived? He should have been sick by now, at twenty-nine. Once a disease was contracted, it was usually fatal in short order. A matter of weeks, which saved on treatment and hospice costs. But some patients lingered, in misery, for months or years.

Some in the Free World, like Daniel, were outliers on the bell curve and lived well into their thirties. For his on-site investigation, they had given him a biohazard suit— uncomfortable for long-term, everyday use, and too expensive for the masses. And not exactly foolproof, as the head lawyer had admitted with a sheepish grin.

Daniel had survived Africa, and in good health. Which was important to the Company. They needed him. His report. Typed on an ancient and secure electric typewriter.

Because in Africa, the Free-World Institute of Health and Disease had identified bubble-less groups in which adults survived as long as they ever had before the newbies, into their fifties and sixties and a few longer than that. At eighty-four, the oldest person in the world was there, in a remote corner of Africa.

That was why Daniel had to go to Africa, the second phase of his research. The primary reason for it, he suspected.

His instructions: study the immune cohorts, identify every place they lived, what they ate, how they interacted with the non-immune villages and towns around them. Try to understand how the immunity works—is it environmental or genetic? Or a combination?

He toured the Orange Company's mines, factories, and other facilities, openly and sometimes even unprotected, and then went into the countryside, dressed as a native. With a specially designed temporary bubble. On loan and no longer with him.

He obtained organ tissue samples, secretly of course, from bribed morticians and doctors. He interviewed and observed dozens of immune villagers. Six months it took, six months of heat and discomfort and threat of kidnapping and death at the hands of the non-bubble rebels. And exposure to a greater concentration of diseases than ever.

And while he was writing his report, Rachel had fallen ill.

The rebels were fueled by resentment and hatred of the bubble people, the "five-percenters" the rebels called them. If they, the forgotten masses, had to die young, said the rebel leader Lumumba, so should everyone share the same fate.

Without regard to wealth.

"All together or not at all," was Lumumba's mantra. His declared goal was to block any exploitation of Africa's resources to support the Free World—and the privileged five percent. Lumumba, the scourge of the Free World, his *nom de guerre* adopted from an African leader supposedly assassinated by agents of the Free World's antecedents.

At one time, it was thought that the earth's moon would replenish the exhausted planet. But not only was it too expensive to supply and maintain and ship the raw materials home, the resources were limited to the most basic: no gold, uranium, or rare earths. Then a meteor swarm had wiped out the first colony and its population.

Mars and the asteroid belt were impractical on a large scale, and mostly unexplored since much of the Company's earnings (and thus the Free World's resources) went to meeting the demand for bubbles—and the seemingly insatiable avarice for material goods and services. For those who could afford them. The five-percenters.

The no-bubble liberals and even a few do-gooder bubble people were clamoring for more, more for the ninety-five percent left unprotected in the disease-ravaged world. But even if the five-percenters were taxed to the limits they could endure and still keep their own bubbles (and baubles), and even if all of the expenditures of the Free World (controlled by the Orange Party and its allies) were directed to producing and servicing personal bubbles, no more than a quarter of the Free World population could be protected—and certainly no more at all in the third and the fourth worlds.

Those with no bubble and no immunity would not just die off. The disease only struck after puberty, and they could still breed before they died. And breed they did, prolifically, though many infants died from old-world causes. In the third and fourth worlds, there were not enough resources to provide even the most basic medical care—and still have bubbles for the five percenters in the Free World.

"Those people," as the Chief called them, or sometimes "those human dregs" (almost all the third and fourth worlds), "always want more, even if they can never have bubbles." They, the dregs, wanted a lot more. And they were in revolt. Committing violent acts of terrorism against the Free World. Destroying every bubble they could.

Daniel's report provided his assessment of the Nigerian "dregs" and options for fighting the terrorists, destroying their habitat, and removing their popular base of support—draining the swamp, the Chief called it. Crucial, the Chief said, because if the Africa resources were threatened, the cost of producing bubbles would skyrocket, and even fewer would be able to afford one in the Free Market.

The Chief and her allies had a solution in mind, so Daniel believed. His research would supply the data and a rationale the Chief could give the One Hundred—the collective body that ran the Orange Party and thus the Free World—and persuade the One Hundred to act. First, they must clear the crucial areas of Africa of all non-immune populations and then replace them with robots and a small and growing cohort of the immunes. To create a "brave new world," the Chief had mockingly called it. She waxed almost poetic about test-tube babies and clones.

They thought he didn't know. But they underestimated his skills, especially his ability to plant listening devices no larger than a flea or speck of lint. That's how he'd heard about the "brave new world."

The Chief was now addressing the two Directors and public relations Vice President who had just returned to the conference room. Telling them that Daniel's report would provide guidance on how to help the Africans, ameliorate their suffering, and even extend their lives. And by benevolent policies tamp down the rebellion.

The microbiology lab was already studying the tissue samples from the immune populations, she said. A team of epidemiologists would visit the immune tribes—there were two of them—to follow up on Daniel's report and conduct further research. The goal: find the source of their immunity and determine how to transfer it to everyone. Give the rebels and the hoi polloi supporting them hope of a remedy, she said, the rebellion will shrivel and die.

It was all a lie.

He had e-dropped the head lawyer, heard what the Chief really intended.

They knew the immunity was genetic, indeed a mélange of genetic mutations that the Orange Company science group had been trying to replicate for years—and failed. DNA engineering at fertilization or in utero had not produced viable specimens. Meanwhile, the immune tribes had multiplied—into thousands of people, maybe as many as 10,000 now. The only way to achieve full immunity would be to interbreed with the tribes and hope that three or five generations afterward your progeny would be immune. Through evolution.

As the Chief talked, Daniel had a thought that almost made him laugh. And what would happen as the immune cohort proliferated? An immune population, a race of black or brown people, in the billions and bubble people and the contaminated masses dwindling into the millions. How would the bubble people be superior then?

With their extravagant displays of wealth? Toys of the rich?

Perhaps the privileged bubble tribe, the five-percenters, would lose, be completely wiped out. Like they were planning to do to the others, the non-immune, the unprotected.

Bubbles could be popped. A bullet, a laser? While there was a quick seal for that, a bubble wasn't armor. The body could still be wounded. And a flame thrower would always work, or a guillotine. Or the infrastructure that supported the entire bubble elite could be destroyed.

Daniel was dismissed. His report on the locations and numbers of the immune tribes in Nigeria had been praised. Invaluable, the Chief said. Nonpareil in the annals of modern scientific research, according to the head lawyer. He would be paid handsomely.

But not enough for a bubble and not in time for Rachel.

So now the Company's eradication of the non-immune in Africa and cultivation of the immune population could begin. And proceed unimpeded once the rebels were wiped out with the most modern biological weapons—using the very diseases that plagued the world already.

The Company had not been able to eliminate the drug-resistant strains, but it had been able to make them more potent, weaponized. And these would supplement the more banal methods of war: fire, blast, radiation, and steel.

They thought their plans were safe, but they were not.

While they believed no other copies of his report existed, none other than the one in the Chief's hands, they were wrong.

As he exited the conference room, he was mulling over his plan. The full document, along with a transcript of the e-dropped conversation between the head lawyer and the Chief, would go out this very afternoon, not just to the rebels but to every media outlet and every political and business leader. Within seconds, it would be copied to every e-box. There were still many who had a conscience. They would balk, even if they were squeamish only at *so many* dying—unnaturally.

A guard stepped out of the shadows in the hallway, and then a second, and another, and another. The guards said nothing. They surrounded him, and two forced his hands behind him and into plastic cuffs as he struggled. Another threw a silencer hood over his head.

He knew the drill. He'd seen it before.

He should have realized. As a bubble-less drone, the five percent could not let him survive. Not with all he knew.

They were moving down the hallway, Daniel wedged between two goons, when from behind came a muffled voice.

Remotely controlled, the hood allowed him to hear and respond when permitted by the controller.

"Daniel." It was the voice of the head lawyer, close by his right ear. "We can't take any chances, Daniel." The voice was soft, placating. "We know your history, we know your life, we know your psychological makeup. And we know about Rachel. We had an alter ego accompany you in Africa, so we know your sympathies. And - we - know what you've been working on."

Daniel twisted around and struggled as hard as he could against the restraining hands and the cuffs. To show the bubble lawyer—to show him what? His shouts of anger and defiance and hatred would not be heard. Not beyond the silencing fabric.

A hand patted him on the shoulder. "It will be gentle with you, and swift, much easier than enduring a newbie virus in the wild. I hate to see this happen. But it's a matter of survival. Survival of the fittest."

Daniel listened calmly now. His protests would not be heard, not here, not ever.

"You have it wrong, Daniel. The threat to us is not from the bubble-less masses like you, but from the immune tribes. What if they spread? Where would that leave us? It really doesn't matter if your message goes out. It may actually help."

As the head lawyer's steps receded down the hall, the realization came to Daniel. His hope dissipated. The e-message would still go out. The rebels could prepare. And among the elite, perhaps those with compassion would stop the eradication of the non-immune masses.

That was what the Chief wanted.

And he wondered, had there ever been a virus from Callisto, or just too many unnecessary people, using up too many resources, growing old, being unproductive since robots provided almost everything the five-percenters required. Better that the masses die young and die quickly. As they did now.

The immune ones were the real threat. If they survived and proliferated and grew old, they would consume resources like swarms of locusts. And prevail. The survival of the fittest. Study them, experiment on them, but never let them be fruitful and multiply.

The End

LOOKING FOR GARY CHEERS

You never know when will be the last time you'll ever see someone. I'm not talking about family or someone you see all the time or someone who dies in your arms. That's another story. In life, there's always a last time, but will you remember it?

The last time I saw Gary Cheers he was working with a Head Start Program at a school in a small North Carolina town on the coast. We talked in the gym while the kids played basketball or volleyball or something like that. It was the year after we graduated from the University of North Carolina at Chapel Hill and went our separate ways, Gary to grad school, me to law school.

I'd driven up the coast from Ocean Drive Beach where I was staying with my girlfriend, and I asked around his hometown until I found him. It didn't take long; only a gas station or convenience store and someone directed me to the school.

What we talked about I don't remember, only the scene with my girlfriend standing to one side and listening. Certainly we talked about what we'd done the past year, Gary at Florida State and me at Duke. He was going for a degree in psychology, one of his many interests in college. We probably talked about the war, about Nixon, about the pits the country was in.

I don't think he was going back to grad school the next semester. Maybe the money. Maybe the threat of the draft and a deferment to teach school was an option. I'm not sure. I was surprised he wasn't going back. Disappointed somehow.

This was three weeks before I left for basic training and ultimately Vietnam—since I'd been drafted while I was in law school. No more deferments. No interest in the Reserves, where a helpful dean had found a couple of open slots.

It was a last idyll at the beach, but for some reason I wanted to go see Gary before I left for the army. Maybe because it was a cloudy day and only a short trip up the coast. I'm sure the girlfriend wasn't impressed with Gary. Wirier and smaller than me, he had short blond hair and a mouse face, and he talked with a funny accent, "aboot" for about, an eastern-shore accent he called it, and pedantically correct. But he was fit and smart and alive with interest in everything around him.

My girlfriend probably wasn't impressed with me either since she dumped me not long after she saw my shaved head, my loss of law-student swagger. Peered into the abyss of war, no light at the end of the tunnel. Or maybe she realized something about me, about us, that I already knew. There was a last, perfunctory goodbye in the rain on the dorm steps, the streetlight glistening on the sidewalk and the bushes by the steps. Shining on her face when she stood on the step above me. Her baby doll dress with a bow in the back. Funny the things you remember.

Older and warier, no longer a working lawyer, I stumbled on her obituary on the internet, no more than a single paragraph. Husband, daughter, memorial service at a funeral home. I didn't find anything else on her, but I'm still curious about her life, what she'd done. The short time it lasted between us, it was good. I remember the last time I saw her.

I've known a few people quite well for a time, or worked with them, and they pass out of my life, and me theirs, and then I hear they've died. A couple of lawyers I worked with on cases, broke bread with in expense account meals and enjoyed their conversation. Liked them. And they died young. A youth minister whom I met at a church camp where I lifeguarded and he was a counselor, and later dined with and served as his subject for a course he was taking on counseling, and I later sought his advice about a girlfriend problem, a high school senior who ran away from an abusive home.

I wondered if my minister friend was gay, in the closet in those days. No women in his life that I could see. We'd gone our separate ways well before I was drafted, but I tried to track him down over the years, even calling the Duke Divinity School. They didn't have a record of where he was, and I didn't follow up. Then in the alumni magazine, I saw his obituary. The memories abide, though, the two of us sitting behind Burl Ives in the Duke Chapel, Handel's *Messiah* rising and washing over us.

Some of what I remember may be wrong. But that's the way I remember it.

Gary was special. Gary was ordinary. Witty. Insecure. Smart.

We spent much time together during our four years at UNC. Friends, roommates, housemates, and competitors in freshman calculus and sophomore zoology, lunches and dinners and beers in bars, bullshit sessions. More than a few lonely Saturday nights—no dates, too bummed out about it to study. Looking for girls to chat up, never finding any at this predominately male bastion, then.

One spring night we set out thumbing, headed for the beach near his hometown, down a lonely two-lane road from Chapel Hill with only a six-pack of beer. Two losers, I was thinking, seeking something, fleeing I don't know what. Headed for utopia, and we didn't make it. Or maybe we did and didn't know it.

I don't remember how far we got under those dark pine trees before we turned back. The beer disappeared faster than any rides appeared.

Years later, back from Vietnam, gainfully employed and owning a car, raising two kids with my wife, I asked a mutual friend, another former housemate, "Tom, you ever hear anything from Gary Cheers?"

"Nope, not since Carolina. Next time I go to the coast, I'll look him up."

Once before, after Vietnam and law school, my new wife and I drove through Gary's little town, and I asked a few people if they knew him, but not a serious effort—just passing through on our way to someplace else. Time pressing us on.

Later I heard that he'd earned a master's degree, or maybe it was that he didn't finish it. Heard that he'd ended up back home, teaching school. Or maybe I imagined all that. I'm sure he was a good teacher, though—curious about everything, eager to share what he'd learned.

I don't think he wanted to go back there—to the small town, a dot on the coastal highway. He had big ambitions, big dreams when I knew him. Wanted to explore the world, do great things. I always thought he'd go far, be a college professor maybe or a doctor or a psychiatrist or something like that. And maybe he did do great things.

During our freshman year, Gary lived across the hall from Johnny of Chowan County, the state peanut capital, as Johnny reminded us. That was the year some redneck threatened to kill me over what I said in a dorm bull session, that I wouldn't care if my daughter dated someone who was black. Long before I had a daughter.

That wasn't Johnny, who always seemed harmless, good-hearted and well-intentioned, friendly. Once at the end of a holiday, on a Sunday night—the memory lingers in part because it was one of those times when you're just back in the pressure cooker of grades and loneliness after a long bus ride, not wanting to be there but needing to be, having to be, missing family or the high school sweetheart you've seen for the last time—and Gary and I were standing outside his dorm room, talking or maybe leaving for the cafeteria, and Johnny pops out of his room with a bowl of peanuts.

Stepping into the corridor, he holds out the bowl. "Like some peanuts?" he says. "Just brought 'em from home. Best in the world."

Another friend from UNC told me later that he and Johnny were in the same unit stateside after basic training. Johnny had volunteered and become a lieutenant—it went to his head, my friend said. My friend and I were draftee peons, which, as former law students—both poor kids on the make until we were waylaid by the draft—was a bitter pill to swallow. In the army, Johnny was the boss, the man, not the genial Johnny we hardly knew at UNC. So my friend said.

Johnny died in Vietnam. Killed by a grenade or booby trap out in some ville in the boonies. His name's on the Wall. Just like Murray's, the upperclassman who sat across from me in study hall in high school.

I can still see him, Johnny, standing in the door to his room, holding out the bowl of peanuts. I think they were raw, or maybe boiled, but not the roasted ones I like. Gary would've remembered.

I recall a few spectacles we attended: a spring bacchanal on the Quad (did we actually have dates?); purple Jesus in a jug (can't remember my date, if I did); protesting the "speaker ban" law, listening to some communist dinosaur (I got bored and left—had to study, Gary stayed to the final yawn). Most performers I don't remember, but the Ramsey Lewis Trio I do.

Gary reveled in it all: politics, civil rights, free speech, esoteric discussions of religion, philosophy, and life—and music. Especially the music. He taught himself to play the guitar—and played and sang. Not that I stayed around to listen. Otis Redding, "Sitting on the Dock of the Bay." When I hear Otis Redding now, I think of Gary. "Watching the tide roll away . . ."

The years go by, and I ask Bob, a former housemate, if he's heard from Gary. Nope, he says. He'll stop by Gary's hometown next time he goes to the coast. My then wife, still my wife now, says it had become an inside joke with us: Bob and Tom and me: looking for Gary Cheers. By this time, I'm making a pretty good living as an oil company lawyer. I'd escaped my small-town roots, though they still grew deep in my gut, and I often went to visit my aging mother when I could schedule her into my travels. Going back there and getting a haircut in my old barbershop, seeing Tom or Bob, eating pulled-pork barbecue, slipping into my Southern accent and lost vocabulary. "Over yonder, you reckon, livin' high on the hog."

I don't know who told me, or when it was. Gary was dead. A brain tumor or something like that. It was probably a half-dozen years after he died that we found out.

The penultimate (a word Gary would use), the penultimate time I saw Gary was at graduation in 1968. My widowed mother, uneducated, not even a grammar school graduate, a millworker, only learning to drive a car after my father died, had driven down to Chapel Hill by herself. My brother had moved to Tennessee with his young family and couldn't make it.

But Gary's whole family was present: mother, father, sisters, baby brother, and all proud enough of Gary to burst. He was the oldest, and this was a big deal for them: first in the family to go to the state university and do well there—all A's and B's, graduating in the top 10% of the class. We were always in competition, and I was probably a bit jealous of his successes. And Gary of mine, I suppose. I went to law school and did okay there, made law journal and all that. I received the letter saying I'd been selected while I was in basic training.

I always expected Gary to excel at what he undertook— and that we would cross paths someday and know we'd each done well in life. Had families who loved us, appreciated us, and we them.

It didn't happen that way, that we ever crossed paths again after those brief minutes in the high school gym in

1969 while the Head Start kids played nearby. But I hope they remember him, and others remember him, as well.

And I wonder, will anyone remember the last time they saw me?

The End

ACROSS THE DIVIDE

"Tomorrow, two thirty," the guy with the car says. "This intersection—and don't be late."

"No sweat, I'll be here." From here, it's another one hundred and twenty miles, miles over back roads he'd have to hitchhike by himself.

The car leaps forward, scratching gravel onto the pavement in front of him. He looks at his watch. It's already after five. In her letter, she said she'd be there, if he could get a pass. But the drill sergeants wouldn't let them leave until late, almost three o'clock this Saturday afternoon. He has an overnight pass, has to make roll call at five p.m. on Sunday.

Across the road there's a Texaco station with a pay phone at the corner. Maybe he should call her. He crosses the road. As he steps onto the drive, a car sweeps by, going north. He enters the phone booth, eyes still on the car, watching it disappear over the rise. Going north, in the direction he wants to go.

The dorm phone rings and rings, but no one answers. It's Saturday night, date night in the Age of Aquarius.

He presses his forehead against the back of his hand, his palm resting on the glass. Once an aspiring scholar of English literature, he still agonizes, broods in the language of Shakespeare: "My love is as a fever, longing still."

She enters the bedroom wearing a white towel around her waist, drying her raven hair with a second white towel. She's clean-scrubbed, red-tinged white, with the hint of a tan line above her small out-turned breasts.

"Will you put some baby oil on me?" she asks. "My skin is dry."

"Where?"

"All over." She drops the towels and lies down on top of the white sheets.

Slamming open the phone booth's door, he hurries across the road. Two more cars roar past, headed north, headed his way. No going back. He's committed. He has to see her.

Thumb out, he waits. No bag, just the civilian clothes and a light jacket he wears against the fall air. No hat, no hair.

Twilight. A lonely two-lane road in South Carolina. Here among the pines, it's already dark, the only sunlight glinting on a silver plane, long rose-white contrail drifting behind it, high in the still-blue sky above the expanse of gloom-filled woods. He breathes in the fall aroma of leaves burning somewhere beyond the trees. Nearby, the cool, damp smells of football nights, of hay and corn stubble, of earth and decay, and Octobers past.

Leaving home, even one not so good, always has a sadness to it. Leaving home in the rain—moving trunks, suitcases, and boxes of books into small rooms and making beds with fresh new sheets and blankets. Leaving to catch a bus, a train, a plane on a Sunday afternoon in autumn when the sky is a brilliant blue and the leaves on the trees are bright yellow against the sky, and some are falling, and some are rustling around your feet as you walk.

Leaving a house after death when all the furniture has been sold, the letters and pictures sorted and packed, and the old cards saved from holidays and birthdays long past thrown in the trash. Looking around at empty rooms, turning out the lights one last time, locking the front door in the dark.

Leaving is something you always remember.

The ladies from the draft board hand each of them a small plastic bag. In it are matches, a four-pack of cigarettes, a toothbrush, gum, and a short pencil and postcard to write home when you get to Basic Training. A plump, white-haired woman—whose daughter he taught to swim—gives him a manila envelope.

"These are your orders," she says. "For the officer when you get there." She steps back and smiles at him. "Have fun."

"Right." He looks straight ahead as he climbs the two steps into the bus.

He finds a seat. Watches as another unwilling warrior saunters down the aisle toward him. This one has long hair to his shoulders and striped pants, in one hand next to his ear a transistor radio playing a local rock station, but everyone can hear the tinny echo—"that deaf, dumb, and blind kid . . ."

Striped pants takes a seat behind him. After a few minutes, he leans forward, hand on the seat back. The radio's still playing.

"Got a light?" he asks, long hair flopping down over one eye, hair that will be gone tomorrow. He reaches out a hand with an unlit cigarette.

"You didn't get a package?"

Striped pants falls back into his seat as the bus lurches forward. "Fuck no," he says. "Don't want any of their shit."

They ride down the highway into the morning sun. The trees reach across the two-lane road to touch tips of branches, their fresh green bathed in a halo of sun-drenched mist that looks deep yellow through the tinted windows. Beyond his reflection in the window, trees, telephone poles, cars, houses flash by—minutes, hours, years.

The news comes on the radio, just loud enough to be annoying. First, from Vietnam, the Pentagon says that 219 American soldiers died in hostile action during the past week. But on a positive note, more than 3000 Viet Cong and North Vietnamese regulars were killed during search and destroy operations. U.S. troop strength will increase another 50,000 by the end of the year, over 500,000 Americans there now, allowing the South Vietnamese time to build up their army and force the communists to the bargaining table. So the Pentagon says. So Nixon says.

He tries not to listen, and the radio station cooperates by starting to break up in bursts of static. Before it's gone, he hears: Judy Garland is dead. "No, this ain't Kansas, Toto," the disc jockey shrieks and then switches to the strains of "Somewhere over the rainbow." As they slip through patches of shadow and sunlight, Judy Garland's voice crackles and fades and dies in the static, and the striped-pants warrior turns off the radio.

A soldier from Fort Gordon, a real soldier—not a trainee like him, offers a lift to just over the North Carolina line. He declines a cigarette, and they speed onward, windows open, in a cool whirlwind of air and eddying smoke. Beyond twilight—into black night.

Brash, buzz-cut blond hair and lean face, the soldier is airborne "all the way." A small blue-flag tattoo graces his flexed bicep. Ashtray full of cigarette butts, cracked windshield, radio blaring, "War, what is it good for?"

"Hey, man, don't you fucking know it!" says the soldier in response to the song. Going home before he ships out. Man/boy, where in six months? Acrid smell of dead cigarettes.

The hitchhiker is not a good soldier, eager to join the fight, never will be. When the lifers are gone, he calls cadence for his platoon marching to chow:

They issued us some jungle boots,

hurrah, hurrah,

they issued us some jungle boots,

so we could run when Charlie shoots,

and we'll all be dead in the winter of '69.

And they believed it.

He stands under a streetlight mounted on a creosote pole near the road, stands next to the pole in a wide circle of light. There's a comforting scent from times lost: walking on railroad ties with his father, waiting by other telephone poles still warm from the sun.

Hungry now, he eats the small pack of Lance crackers in his jacket pocket. All the food he has.

At the University, he took a course in Southern literature with all its dreamscapes and poetic lies. "O lost and by the wind grieved."* What has he lost? Drudgery in the library, long hours of research and writing footnotes. Figuring out how to pay for the next semester. The best romance he ever had. No, not romance. The best sex.

She lies on the bed, propped up on her elbows, chin in her palm, studying anthropology for summer school. The white sheet is pulled up to her waist, leaving naked brown back and shoulders from the waist up.

He lies on his side next to her, rubbing her back.

"What does bipedal mean?" she asks.

"What?" He runs his fingers down her spine from the neck to just above the sheet and along the sharp tan line. He leaves for Basic Training in a week.

"B-i-p-e-d-a-l, what does it mean?"

"Upright, on two legs." He leans over, places his head on the small of her back, then kisses the imaginary line where he had run his fingers. She shivers.

"You're making it so-o-o hard to concentrate."

"For you?"

"Just wait 'til I finish this."

He looks down at her tan back and dark hair. "Lithe." L-i-t-h-e. Her tan back against the white sheet, the form of her buttocks and her legs extending under the sheet to the crumpled-up blue bedspread at the foot of the bed.

"Promise me . . ." He stops.

"Promise you what?"

"While I'm gone, date and all that, but don't sleep with anyone else."

---

*Thomas Wolfe, *Look Homeward Angel.*

"I hadn't planned on it." She rolls over, puts her arms around his neck, and kisses him as he leans across her body, still flushed from the afternoon sun.

He finishes the last cracker and sticks out his thumb at an old Chevy pickup. It slowly coasts past and rattles to a stop beyond the fringe of light. He runs over, and an old woman opens the passenger door, tells him to get into the cab with her and Earl. Her name is Annie, or did she say "Auntie"? She reminds him of his grandmother, small round face, hair pulled back in a gray bun, black print dress with small white flowers—Grandma dead now almost fifteen years, mind gone years before. The same musty smell of snuff and bath powders and age.

Earl looks like Tom Joad grown old—weather-beaten wrinkled face, bib overalls, and beat-up gray fedora, bent brim in front. Tom Joad hunched forward in great earnestness, eying the dark headlight-slashed road ahead over the steering wheel. A harmonica dangles by an elastic cord wrapped twice around the visor above the steering wheel.

"Only goin' a short piece up the road heah to the home place," Earl says.

"We knowed you was a soldier by the way you looked," she says.

Their son had been a soldier, too, in the last war. But they don't say any more about him, and he doesn't ask because of the way her voice drops and her face follows it down.

"Mind if we have a little music?" Earl asks and lifts his eyes from the road to the harmonica.

"No, no, not at all," he says. He squeezes closer to the door and hangs on to the handle. Checks the lock.

The old man bats at the harmonica with a gnarled hand, grabs it on the second swing back, and pulls it to his mouth. He plays, sometimes with one hand, sometimes with two, while bracing the steering wheel with his knees, driving slowly, other traffic whooshing around them, rocking the truck. And she sings. "She'll be comin' around the mountain when she comes," and "Oh do you remember sweet Betsy from Pike," only a verse or two of each, and claps her hands while Earl plays a ragged, intermittent accompaniment. And gospel tunes, "In the sweet by and by." And then, the harmonica swaying above the old man's head, they sing together, "Amazing grace, how sweet the sound," and Annie, or Auntie, sings by herself, hands clasped in her lap, "Softly and tenderly Jesus is calling, calling for you and for me. Come ho-me, come ho-o-ome, ye who are weary, come ho-ome."

All is peaceful and safe in the warm cocoon of this rattling Chevy pickup truck on a dark North Carolina road. Simple folk, their son was a soldier, too.

They turn off the blacktop onto a dirt road leading into a forest of pines and stop. Invite him home with them, to sup. Sparse victuals, she says—fried ham, turnip greens, cornbread, but enough for all of them.

"Come on spend the night, son. Don't be out heah in no dark."

But no. He has to move on. He looks at his watch—almost eight, but he can make it in a couple of hours. Too late now to turn back. Maybe she'll be there. Saturday night? She said to come if he could. Maybe he can leave her a note if she's not there and they can meet in the morning, spend some time together.

Doubt wars with images from the spring.

It's late afternoon, after a visit to the beach and a swim in the ocean. He starts to rub baby oil on her but doesn't get beyond her back and one leg before they roll over into the middle of the bed. The sun through the thin curtains suffuses the room in a low pleasant light.

She stops moving, her fingernails digging into his back, and pulls him down tight against her breasts. Her legs slide down past his hips.

"Take it off." Her voice is urgent, her breathing fast and shallow.

He pushes up on his hands and stares down at her. "What? Take what off."

"The rubber. Take it off. I want to feel you . . ."

"We can't . . ."

"I want to feel you go off."

He sinks down, his chest pressed to her bare breasts. He says in a quiet voice, "What if you get pregnant? I can't get married . . . I can't marry you."

She drops her legs and clutches at his sides, almost panting. "I don't care. Just take it off." Then she pushes him away, and he does what she wants, removes the condom, and throws it over the edge of the bed.

Maybe she'll sneak out of the dorm after curfew. She would have before Judy Garland died and he took the long bus ride. To get his head shaved.

 He must go on. He thanks the old couple and gets out of the truck, into the chill fall air, into the night, out among the towering pines.

In front of him lies a lonely two-lane blacktop road, a tunnel through a forest of pine trees rooted in the sandy soil of the coastal plain. He must go on, on to Chapel Hill, up the road into the rolling Piedmont hills, hills covered with maples and giant oaks with red and yellow fall leaves, not the dark menacing pines of the lowlands, going to the University where he once was, and she still is.

The last time he saw her was in Basic Training. There had been only a few letters and a couple of phone calls, standing in line for the pay phone, dropping in dimes and quarters. But she said she would come when he got a pass.

So he waits for her outside the Orderly Room as the sun goes down. He feels desperate, no longer just a physical, sexual need, but something more. Loneliness? Love? Despair? "O lost and by the wind grieved."

For a trainee, there's only a four-hour pass on a Saturday night, and then only if he has his shit together for the week. And he does.

What can they do in four hours, now nearer three? He thought about getting a room. He's never rented a motel room by the hour. But where? He doesn't know Fayetteville, North Carolina—has never been there. Only Fort Bragg, six weeks inside this expanse of sand, red dirt, pines, and scrub oaks, crisscrossed by asphalt roads, full of callow trainees and jaded veterans, military trucks and jeeps, barracks and rifle ranges.

Everyone else with a pass has already gone, most clutching girlfriends and wives. Conjugal visits—off to motels or maybe a secluded spot under the pine trees, copulating in cars. Maybe to dinner.

Finally she comes, driving her blue Mustang into the parking lot from the main road, the sun low in the sky, casting long shadows through the pines on the other side of the lot. She gets out and floats across the asphalt in her sleeveless white dress, thigh length above bare, tan legs— drifting like a specter, a phantasm, in the slanting sunlight, dark hair gleaming. She looks great.

Going past the Orderly Room toward her, he hears the trainees on police call, without overnight passes, whistling. "Hey, babe, come to poppa. Got somethin' here for ya." Then the drill sergeant shuts them up and reserves the sight for himself.

They meet in the parking lot, hug, kiss. The feel of her body pressed to his, the taste of her lips, her mouth, her perfume, sweet and rich, blended by perspiration with the subtle smell of her skin, makes every cell in his body yearn for her.

They lock arms around each other's waist and walk to the car. He's in dress Khakis, and he takes off his garrison cap, a cunt cap, the lifers call it.

"You don't have any hair," she says. Surprise? Shock?

"I told you they keep it shaved off." He looks at his wristwatch, which is starting to corrode from his crawling through rain puddles and mud. "You're late."

"It took longer than I thought. Over two hours to get here."

"It's almost seven-thirty. I have to be back by ten." He pauses. "We could get a room."

"Not now. I'm hungry . . . I haven't eaten anything since breakfast."

"Okay. Maybe we can find something in town." Where he's never been.

She's the only nourishment he wants, needs; his every sensory receptor is popping, and he's hornier than he can ever remember being in his whole life.

Maybe later? he thinks, but lets it go—for now.

She drives. He's not allowed to, doesn't even have a driver's license at Basic Training. He obeys rules, fears punishment.

They get lost on their way off the base. He only knows the roads used for the ten-mile hikes and marching to the rifle range. They ride around on strange asphalt byways, past the rifle ranges, past parade grounds, barracks, and buildings he's never seen before, and down the fence line next to the runway for the airfield. He hears the roar of C-130s taking off. Smells jet fuel and pine sap.

Finally, they're on the main road—Bragg Boulevard—and it's after 8:00pm. Less than two hours left. No room tonight, no soft bed and full length of warm nakedness entwined together. Maybe a dark spot off the road? But where?

Now there's traffic, lots of it, cars moving slowly, then stopped, not moving at all. They talk and wait to move and talk some more. Irritating banalities. He lusts, looking at her tan arms and shoulders set off against the white dress, and the legs—white dress pulled up high on her thighs as she presses the clutch, downshifts, and brakes to a stop. As she changes gears again, he reaches across the console and gently lays his hand on her bare thigh.

Both maneuvers completed, hers and his, she takes his hand and moves it back across to his leg, leaving her hand on his thigh and saying, "Don't do that. I have to drive. This traffic's bad." She squeezes his leg, then removes her hand to shift into third as the cars in front surge forward. It's twilight, and the lights encasing the used car lots, pawnshops, and gas stations along the road have blinked on.

"Let's just stop somewhere and make out," he says brightly.

"Don't be silly."

Eight-thirty and they don't seem to be anywhere near downtown. How many miles can it be? But the traffic still plods forward.

"Let's just go eat somewhere . . . along here," he says. "There's a Shoney's over there." He points.

She pulls the car into the Shoney's and parks in a dark corner at the back. They lean across the console and engage in a long, deep kiss, hands moving over each other's body— but she breaks away when he runs his fingers along the inside of her thigh.

"Let's go," she says. "I'm hungry." She turns away and opens the door.

The restaurant is teeming with sweaty bodies. Deafening noise: kids wailing, dishes breaking, patrons shouting across tables. Food on the floor, glacial service, hamburger and ice cream sundaes, and it's 9:20 by the time the check arrives, and he pays. Only thing to do is start back to base.

More traffic. After a few wrong turns and directions from an MP, who examines his pass, they reach Training Company B's parking lot at 2155 hours. Time only for a four-minute kiss and feeling that body he so needs through the fabric and briefly underneath the dress before he sprints to the Orderly Room. He waves, and the car moves toward the road. She waves back—he thinks. It's too dark to see.

He waits a long time for another ride, but no one stops. He walks to a Gulf station, where he buys a Coke and gets a lift from two high school boys filling the tank of an old Dodge Charger, a muscle car, boys on the prowl for girls, all-American boys with Beatles haircuts and freckles turned to pimples and English Leather aftershave, just riding around on a Saturday night, no hope of finding any girls now, if there ever was, and—why not? Sure, they'll take him up the road a ways. The one on the passenger side pulls his seat forward, and he climbs in the back.

Leaning up, forearm resting on the seatback, he tells them, shouts over the radio racket, about Basic Training, the power and kick of the M-14, the scrawny kid who dropped the grenade in the bunker. The grizzly bear of a drill sergeant tossing the kid out and scrambling over the wall after him, two seconds before the explosion.

"Wow!" the one says, the passenger. The radio now soft.

He watches the speedometer needle. Sixty, seventy, eighty. The car careens around a curve and swerves back into its lane to avoid the huge lights of an oncoming semi-truck. Showing him that they are brave, fearless, reckless of death, showing him how to take life now that he may soon be dead in a rice paddy half a world away.

On a straight stretch, going uphill at eighty-five, the car coughs and balks, and the driver, the quiet one, backs off to seventy. They deposit him twenty miles farther up the road, deep in the dark piney woods, turn and roar away, red taillights receding into the night.

Now it's ten o'clock and miles to go. Can't go back. He hugs his jacket to his thin body. The day had been warm, a sunny, Indian-summer day, but now it's cold. He stands under an old-style streetlamp, a single bulb beneath a metal reflector. Intersection with a county road. Thumb out. Not many cars pass now, not at this hour, and most of those speed up when they see him.

Finally. A big car with bright double headlights approaches and glides to a stop beside him under the streetlamp—a new Ford Thunderbird, not the sleek sports car, but the new expanded 1969 version. Lights come on inside as the driver reaches across and opens the door for him to get in. Leather bucket seats. Padded center console. The dashboard glows with lights like the bridge of a spaceship, limning a heavyset man, white shirt, tie undone, black-rim glasses, lots of well-groomed hair. A deodorant or aftershave, pleasingly subtle like a fine perfume.

Pleasant soothing voice. "Where you goin', sport?"

He tells the man and gets in. The car glides smoothly onto the highway and accelerates, pushing its new passenger back in the soft leather seat. Instrumental late-night music plays on the radio, not too loud, not too soft, relaxing.

"You a soldier?" The resonating voice of a preacher or radio announcer.

"Yes sir."

"Could tell from your hair. Or lack of it. So, why are ya out this time of night? It's a little late."

Tells him he's going to see his girl and got a late start.

"She expectin' ya?"

He tells him yes . . . then no, not now, and the man is silent. Asks if the music is okay.

"Sure," he answers.

They're on a straight stretch of road, and the man turns his head to stare at him. Looks him up and down. His brow wrinkles with concern.

"You're not dressed for this weather, sport. Gettin' chilly out."

"I'm warm enough." He tugs at the zipper on the thin jacket. "Didn't expect to be out this late." Pauses. Shrugs. "It's all the civilian clothes I have down there."

Silence settles between them as the pine trees along the road slip by in the broad beam of the headlights. An ad comes on the radio and the man lowers the volume. There's only the hum of wheels on pavement and the engine's throaty growl when the big car accelerates up another low hill into the Carolina Piedmont.

"You ever been with a man?" the heavyset man asks, leaning his elbow on the center console and glancing over at him again.

"What?"

"You know, had sex with a man?"

He's surprised, shocked, frightened. Doesn't know what to say. Can't jump out at this speed. So he says, "no."

"Look," the man says—hasn't offered his name, and he hasn't said his own—"I'm goin' to Raleigh. Why don't ya come with me, and we'll get a room at the Sir Walter for the night."

"Let me out," he says. They're on a dark section of the two-lane road, and no cars are behind them. None have gone past from the other direction in a long time. No houses. Just pine trees.

"It's okay if ya don't want to do anything," the man says, his fingers clicking and releasing the catch on the console between the seats. "But it's almost midnight, and you won't get to see your girl tonight anyway . . . You can have a place to sleep."

"No thanks," he says. "I just want out." He draws in his breath. "Now . . . Please."

"But there's nuthin here. No houses. No service station for miles. Nuthin . . . Just forget what I said." The man sits up straight, clicks open the console, lifts it slightly, and then snaps it shut.

"That's okay," he says. "There's a picnic area. Just let me out there." He points to a sign in the penumbra of the headlights. White outline of a picnic table on a dark background. One mile.

"You may not get another ride tonight, sport. I'm not goin' to do anything to ya."

"Look, all I want is to get out at that picnic area."

They're almost to the pullout next to the table. The man pumps the brakes, and the tires squeal as the car jerks off the road, onto dirt and gravel.

He unlocks the passenger door and has it open before the car stops.

"Thanks," he says and gets out.

The man leans across the passenger seat and says, "Sure you won't—"

He shuts the door and walks back down the shoulder of the road in the direction from which they came. Behind him, the car slowly creeps out of the pullout and onto the asphalt, then edges forward, not accelerating, up a low hill.

Doubling back, he goes past the cement picnic table to the edge of the trees, where he stops to watch. At the top of the hill, the big car pulls off the road to the right side and swings in an arc across to the other lane.

He sees the headlights coming down the hill, back toward him. He darts in among the trees behind the cement table, down a short embankment, and stops, listens. Hears the soft purring of the big Thunderbird as it goes by, slowly—then silence.

He waits. After ten minutes or so he picks his way among the trees and bushes to the forest boundary of the picnic area and stares out at the empty road. A half-moon has risen over the pines, and in the dim light he can see the white cement table in the narrow clearing between the road and trees.

He waits. Then he sidles across the grassy area around the table to the asphalt. All he sees is empty road and pine trees. It's after midnight.

He waits. No cars. What if the man comes back? He was going in the wrong direction for Raleigh, where he said he was going.

The air is dank, heavy. A lone frog or insect gives a low rasping, modulating call, then stops abruptly. The trees whisper above him. Still no cars.

He's tired, sleepy, hungry, cold. He curls up on the bare ground beneath the picnic table against one of the cement legs, grabbing his arms and hugging his thin jacket around him. The wide-spread table legs conceal him from the road, except right in front, and protect him from the breeze that has picked up, rustling the bushes and the needles in the pine trees around the clearing.

A car with a broken muffler roars by, and he starts awake, watches, his eyes wide, as the headlights sweep past, until the sound fades into silence. He tries to go back to sleep, his mind plagued with dark thoughts.

He opens his eyes. In the dull, nearly-dawn light, he can see the beer cans and paper trash on the ground around the picnic table—waxy McDonald's wrappers, crushed cups, and white paper napkins—and can make out the outline of the trees. Down through the woods, fine wisps of ground fog rise among the pines. He takes off his glasses, closes his eyes—a minute . . . two . . . dozes—then puts his glasses back on, unbends, stands, and places one hand on the concrete tabletop. His hand comes away wet. Dew. Dew in the cool fresh morning. Dew glistening on the grass beside the table. He wipes his hands on his civilian slacks and looks up to see the sunlight hitting the tops of the pines.

A beautiful yellow morning, a new day.

"Good morning, star shine." The song on the radio when they drove through another pine forest on an early spring morning.

But what if she's not there?

He urinates behind a sun-topped pine tree and starts walking—until he catches a ride with a black minister in a too-large polyester suit and a white shirt. A little girl in a bleach-clean white dress—solemn face, pigtails tied with red ribbons—rides in the back seat. Headed to church. Only a mile or two, but they couldn't just leave him out there, all alone in that lonely spot.

The minister tells him how far it is to Chapel Hill, twenty more miles, and offers him a stick of spearmint gum in a mint-green wrapper. In a corner of the rear-view mirror, he sees the face of the little girl in the back seat, sees that she is staring wide-eyed at him, his skull-like profile, the white soldier, turned toward her father. Along with the mint taste of the gum, there's a fragrance of Sundays that he knows, that he has known almost from birth: of sun-dried clothes, freshly ironed, a lemon scent of Octagon soap.

From a pay phone at the Esso station across from the Mount Hebron Salvation Tabernacle of the Lord, he calls Fred, an old friend—now in law school at the University—and begs for a ride. Fred, half asleep, says he's hung over and can't come that far. Catch another ride and he'll meet him outside Chapel Hill, at the Howard Johnson's where they used to go for breakfast. Before Judy Garland died.

He looks up to open the phone booth door and sees the big Thunderbird easing off the road and gliding toward him. It's two-tone, tan-and-white, which he couldn't see the night before. The Esso station is closed, but it's daylight, and he feels no fear. Nor anger. Just numb resentment. He turns and walks in the opposite direction, toward the highway, where a few cars are coming and going by now.

Behind him, the Thunderbird's engine goes quiet, idling. The car door opens.

He keeps walking away, and the man calls out.

"I was worried about ya, sport. I went back, last night . . . but you were gone. I couldn't just leave you like that. Been all over looking for ya. Just in case . . ." The voice trails off.

He keeps on walking.

"I won't hurt ya. That's not . . . I'm not . . . I'm not like that. I—I'm sorry. I just want to help ya get there . . . go see your girl. If you'll let me."

He stops and turns. They must be thirty or forty yards apart. The man has his arms raised out to his side, as if in supplication. He doesn't look as big as he had seemed. Overweight and ordinary and anxious is how he seems now. Middle-aged.

"I'll take ya there. Let me help you, fella . . . I *want* to help *you.*"

He looks around. There's no one else there but them and, across the road, the congregation inside the small church. A hymn, accompanied by an off-key piano, rises in the quiet morning air. "Blessed assurance, Jesus is mine . . ."

"Okay," he says. He nods. He could warn the man, tell him not to try anything. But he doesn't have to. He knows the man will take him where he wants to go. But his girl won't be there.

Fred chortles at the tale of his journey, which doesn't include the man in the Thunderbird. He chides him about his quixotic quest for Dulcinea, whom he also knows, but not yet in the biblical sense. She's probably moved on to new beds, he sagely offers. Not going to waste her time on a hairless army freak. Calls him a dumb ass. Fred never minces words. Tells it like it is. Fred smells like stale beer and cigarettes and clothes he took back out of the hamper this morning.

From the restaurant, he calls the dorm again. A strange voice answers. After long minutes, her roommate comes to the phone and tells him she's gone for the weekend, visiting friends, in Greensboro or someplace like that.

But she said she'd be there.

He hangs up, pounds the wall with his fist, and thinks. Fred's right. What a dumb fucking idea.

"Freddy, good friend, can you give me a lift to Cheraw, South Carolina?"

"Hey, what are friends for? Let's go," says Fred.

And they go. Back down the road he had come up in the dark, not many hours before—not the shortest or best way, Fred says—but he wants to see it in the daylight. Past the rest area, now spackled with sunlight and exuding warmth. Past the decrepit country filling stations with dirt and gravel drives, broken signs, and antique pumps, Texaco, Esso, Gulf, closed for Sunday, a day of rest.

He now sees—interspersed among the pines—dozens and dozens of dogwoods, maples, and oaks, their leaves turning red and yellow and mauve.

A beautiful fall Sunday afternoon. A beautiful day for a ride through the Carolina forests of green pines and color-doused hardwoods, flashing by in sunlight that dances and shimmers on the car's windows. Warms the body, soothes the soul.

End

MICK

In the wee hours of the morning, ghosts move restlessly through the old colonial villa. Most are flesh, blood, and bone, with livers half-pickled by Jack Daniels. Private Becker, dead sober, has fire watch. It's easy duty: monitor the radio and phone, wake the tower guards, but mainly just stay awake.

The last night patrol has returned—long after its shift should have ended—and the next tower guard is clear of his bunk. The light in the Operations Room, Sergeant Beadle's domain during the day, is dim, and Becker huddles under a desk lamp to read. The English major, a fellow conscript, had shoved Kafka's *The Trial* into his hands and said, "Read this. You'll understand."

As he turns the page, light reflects from the thick lens in his black-rimmed glasses. Short, squat Becker has a mop of unruly black hair that pushes the limits of military regulations even in these lax times. Times worthy of Kafka, to whom Becker already feels a strong kinship. Becker is a weigher of molecules, a watcher of turning wheels.

When Becker looks up, the reflected light plays across the bullet-shaped head and short-cropped hair of a big oval-faced sergeant, three stripes, a buck sergeant, just down from My Tho and pulling temporary night duty before moving on to his next post. He sits on the other side of the desk, filling out a form report. He rarely speaks, doesn't joke.

One of the villa's ghosts bursts into the room from the hallway. The First Sergeant, followed by his retainers: Sergeant Connors from the Motor Pool, Smithy the Mess Sergeant, and Sergeant Hayes. The First Sergeant, red-faced, wearing fatigue trousers and an olive-drab t-shirt, looks around, glaring wild-eyed. Then he staggers over to the desk.

"Not one of those goddamn gooks is to bring a fucking bicycle in here," he shouts at the buck sergeant and Becker. The buck sergeant nods but doesn't say anything. Becker just stares. Top must be talking about the old papa-san and the other Vietnamese who work in the compound.

"Never! You fucking hear me! Never!" The First Sergeant rocks forward over the desk, releasing a blast of foul air and producing a shadow monster across the ceiling from the lamp on the desk.

He's quiet for a moment, then turns to his entourage and waves one arm back toward the desk. "You can tell Mick to do something and he'll fucking do it."

He starts to walk away, a big man with slightly stooped shoulders—not a military bearing, but a man long in the military. He has small sharp eyes under heavy dark eyebrows focused down an aquiline nose. Narrow, truncated head, burr haircut, and puffy red face.

Then he turns back. "Don't ever try anything foolish with me or I'll bust your ass—with this." He holds up his right fist and extends it toward the buck sergeant. He ignores Becker, like he's not even there.

"You see these knuckles?" Top says. He drops his hand onto the gray metal desk, knuckles up—red, hard, and raw looking. "You see 'em, huh?"

"Uh huh," the buck sergeant says and nods slowly.

"Just don't ever go against me."

The First Sergeant stands up straight, raising his shoulders and rolling them forward. "Know karate, huh?"

"No, I just—"

"You see that hand." The First Sergeant's harsh voice cuts through the buck sergeant's quiet New England accent. He holds up his left hand and shakes it in the air. "Weak." He staggers and catches the corner of the desk with the hand he had held up.

"This one's the strong one." He holds up his right hand, clenched in a fist. He twists around and with his fist slams the side of a gray metal filing cabinet, a crashing blow, denting the side and rocking the cabinet back and forth.

"Two knuckles. That's all it takes. Two fucking knuckles." He pauses and glares at the buck sergeant. "Five more months and you'll make E-6, Mick. Just get rid of that goddamn bracelet." He points to a woven black bracelet on the buck sergeant's broad wrist.

"Top, I can't get rid of the bracelet." Mick shakes his head and stares up at Top. "I'll wear it as long as I'm over here. A Montagnard gave it to me when I was a roadrunner—"

"You mean ya bought it at the fucking PX."

"No, First Sergeant, I didn't." He speaks softly but clearly. The only light comes from the lamp on the desk, and the First Sergeant looms above it. "It was given to me by a Montagnard when I was a roadrunner in the highlands . . . I won't take it off while I'm here."

The supporting cast hovers in the shadows by the door.

"Good!" The First Sergeant booms, staggering backward. "If it was given to you, then you're authorized to wear it."

He turns and looks at his audience in triumph. They smile and nod and move toward the door, Hayes in front. It's clear to Becker they want to leave.

Top is almost out the door with his crew when he turns and comes back. He stumbles to a stop beside the desk and leans over it, casting a huge shadow on the ceiling and the walls behind him. He waves a meaty finger in the buck sergeant's face.

"Trim that goddamn mustache." Loud, but not quite a shout.

"I just trimmed it today, Top."

"Goddamn it, if you want E-6, trim it again. You're not authorized any hair below the corners of your mouth."

The buck sergeant doesn't say anything, but the muscles in his lean jaw work up and down. Becker could be a speck of dust floating in front of the lamp for all the First Sergeant cares.

"You'll be okay, Mick," Top says, "just don't try any goddamn foolishness." Top straightens up, the shadows shrinking behind him.

Becker has lasting images of Top, a palimpsest with layers over this one: Top at his desk, head down, showing close-cropped red hair cut like a hairbrush, ignoring him; Top shouting at him to get his head out of his ass; Top under his breath to the CO's back, "you fucking black-ass nigger;" and Top under the stairs, during the mortar attack. On his knees, trembling, hands clutched over his head. Near him, Becker attempts to lace his boots, his hands shaking so hard that he can't. Wrapping the laces around his ankles, he ties them and runs to get his M-16 and bandoliers of ammo, while Hayes puts his arm around Top and leads him off.

This time, Top reaches the outside hallway before he barges back inside—past his loyal troop, none of whom try to stop him. The buck sergeant has lifted a small blue Testament off the desk and started to open it.

"Readin' the Bible, too!" The First Sergeant teeters in the middle of the room, his hands on his hips. "Caught ya." He shifts sideways in a slow dance step. "You scared or religious?"

"I'm religious."

"I'm fucking religious, too. Any goddamn time you feel like it, son, you just come on to my room and we'll talk about the good Lord."

The buck sergeant doesn't say anything, nods his head, and lays the Testament face down on the desk. Top raises his hand, shaking his index finger in the air.

"But the next time I catch some motherfucking NCO runnin' to get some goddamn beads, I'm gonna court-martial the bastard." He stumbles to one side and drops his hand for balance. "You know who I'm talkin' about, don't ya? . . . Don't ya, Mick?"

He turns without waiting for an answer and lunges through the door, held open by one of his retainers. He repeats as he exits, "Yeah, I'm gonna court-martial the bastard."

The room is silent. Neither Becker nor Mick, the buck sergeant, says anything. Becker, his book open flat under the lamp, glances over at Mick, sending glimmers of reflected light across the other man's face, unremarkable except for its oval shape.

Mick shakes his head, his mouth drawn into a tight smile under his neatly trimmed mustache. As Becker goes back to reading Kafka, the sergeant reaches into his fatigue pocket and takes out a rosary. He holds it in one hand above the desk, in a gray edge of light, and moves it through his fingers, clicking the beads together. Driving the ghosts away.

The End

VIETNAM STORY
(A DRAFTEE'S LAMENT)

Looking back on Nam, he sometimes thinks he specialized in brains—sprayed, scrambled, and over easy. Thank God, he tells his son, I was spared the mangled legs, spilled guts, and sucking chest wounds of combat. And I didn't actually see the boy-san bisected by the American deuce-and-a-half, only caught a glimpse of the body on a gurney. Just brains—no longer thinking, plotting, and planning; no longer transmitting, receiving, processing—just dead, silent organic matter left to decay and turn to fetid mush, food for maggots and worms.

Then there was the sickness and the insanity—American GIs and Vietnamese Rangers filled with anger and hatred and booze. But it was an insane time and an insane war—fueled by falsehood, illusion, and corruption. A few did the fighting, killing, and dying, supported by others whose fervent hope was to avoid all that.

It was "the Sixties," an era of death, revolution, and destruction. A time of clichés: free love, flower children, peace signs; a time of demonstrations, race riots, Mary Jane, and LSD. Hippies and yippies. The sexual revolution: what once was hidden is now disclosed, exposed, out. From Peyton Place to Masters and Johnson. The raid on the Stonewall Inn in Greenwich Village starts the gay liberation movement—after Judy Garland dies.

The Sixties, a time of prosperity. A time when the rich do what they do best—get richer, spend money, and remain above it all, removed from the common weal unless slumming suits their whim.

Let them eat cake because, in your heart, you know Goldwater's right.

A time when Jim Crow dies, or maybe not, and Civil Rights become the law, if not the fact, of the land. An explosion of education and knowledge. A landing on the moon. Discoveries and wealth. Color Television. Medicare, Medicaid, and Head Start. The War on Poverty.

A time of assassination. John F. Kennedy in Dallas, Lee Harvey Oswald—live on national television, Medgar Evers in his own driveway, Martin Luther King in Memphis, Bobby Kennedy in an L.A. hotel kitchen. The power of the gun to jolt history, but not to change its course. Maybe.

A time for gratuitous killing. Children in a church. Civil rights workers—beaten, shot, buried in an earthen dam, or left in the street. Charles Whitman kills fourteen, wounds thirty from the University of Texas tower. National Guardsmen at Kent State; police at Jackson State. Riots—Watts, Detroit, Newark, Washington, DC. Cities burn, the already destitute suffer, and politicians wring their hands.

Let them eat cake.

Vietnam: images of helicopters, body bags, Tet, monks burning, cities destroyed. A naked girl, blistered by napalm, running down a road, fire and smoke from the bombs billowing up behind her. A police chief holding a gun to a prisoner's head and blowing his brains out. My Lai: GIs enraged, run amuck, hundreds die and no one can stop it. Viet Cong executions at Hue, trumped in time by the CIA. Phoenix: A secret program to assassinate thousands of suspected Vietnamese communists and collaborators—no trial, no proof, just a body count.

For what results?

All of this has happened before. It is no different this time, except for the pictures—and television, in real-time—and

Americans have the money and leisure to consume it all in great quantities over their evening meals.

They have not yet become jaded, inoculated, immunized, accustomed to it. But they will. And it will happen again, different only in time and manner.

Is the picture on television real? It's more than just Words. Execute a bound prisoner in front of the camera. Do we care? Burn a village; kill the old men, women, and children. Do we care? The evil enemy didn't do that—oh, but they do worse. But one of our own did that. We did that. Stress of battle. Payback for their atrocities. Free Lieutenant Calley! He's only a scapegoat. An aberration. An American war criminal? No such thing. We must defeat the godless communists by any means; therefore, extremism in defense of liberty is no vice. The end is just. We had to destroy the "ville" to save it.

Pictures, hard to ignore, but with practice we succeed, rationalize, explain. Governments learn—control the access, manipulate the cameras, own the owners, buy off and co-opt the messengers. Override. **You are with us or against us**. "And God is on our side."

Gott mit uns!

We were there, he says, we saw what it was. Back in the "real world," halfway around the world, everyone else saw only what they wanted to see, believed only what they wanted to believe, and pretended we were only images on a television screen. Then they forgot about us. Now they wish we would just go away, quietly, softly, "gentle into that good night."[*]

Leaving home—ritual of youth, rite of passage, an unmarked event. Every young man and woman does it—in one way or another—some looking backward, others never looking back, some hesitating, others running.

Leaving home for war. Young men going forth from the hearth, leaving the plow, leaving the land, leaving kith and

[*] Dylan Thomas, '*Do not go gentle into that good night.*'

kin. From the Age of Bronze and before. And after. Leaving mothers and wives behind to fear, to grieve—some to forget too soon. And now young women, as well as young men.

The Twentieth Century spawned war after war, the elements of the scene never changing: young men leaving home to go kill other young men—moved across the map by the gnarled fingers of old men playing sterile games—spilling millions of gallons of blood to soak foreign soils. Vietnam, just one more.

The bus will leave from the Greyhound station at 7:00am. Ex-grad student, Phi Beta Kappa, draftee, he eats breakfast sitting at the yellow Formica-top table under a bare 100-watt light bulb. It is still dark outside. The scrambled eggs are dry and the toast a little burnt. His mother stands looking out the dark window above the white kitchen sink, mechanically washing cups and plates and placing them in the drainer, watching the limbs of the maple outside the window become visible in the new light of the June day.

He shaves, brushes his teeth, and throws a change of underwear and a shaving kit into his brown, fake-leather bag—blue Carolina stickers on the side. He tosses in a paperback and then his army induction notice on top. "Greetings from the President of the United States." He looks down at the bag, thinking about what else he may need, thinking about his uncle's battered old sea trunk sitting at the top of the stairs in the attic. The only thing it holds now is the large burial flag, folded in a neat triangle in the bottom, where it has lain since 1946, the body buried in a foreign grave until then.

He hugs the small white-haired woman, a widow these long years, and walks out the door. She will leave for work at the shirt mill—for minimum wage, no benefits—not long after he goes. If she's been crying, he doesn't see it. She gives a sob when he hugs her, just one. "Take care of yourself, Mother," he says. "I'll be fine." She nods and clutches his arm. Neither says, "I love you." Neither has to.

He steps across last year's date etched in the concrete step, walks past a shrub he's seen flower as long as he can remember, past the red maple tree next to the street, and down the broken sidewalk. The half-empty bag bounces off his leg as he walks.

It is a fine June morning. The air is cool. A thin mist drifts over the new-mown lawn. The sun touches the top of the tall pecan tree in the yard, turning the green leaves yellow. It's only a short walk to the bus station, and he doesn't look back at the end of the street. No one is watching him go.

At the bus station, the members of the local draft board send them off, the young men they have selected to serve their country, whether they want to or not. The bus station has a grease-stained drive under a high canopy next to the waiting room, where men and women have sat on wooden benches and waited to depart for three wars now. Next door is the City News Stand, where he has bought a Sunday newspaper, comic books, and pulp novels for almost all his life, it seems.

In the blink of an eye, it seems now, the inductees of varied backgrounds, most not privileged enough to join the National Guard or Reserves or have a family doctor certify some obscure physical condition or deformity that avoids the draft, are on board and waiting for their lives to change forever. After this, nothing will be the same as before, over a cliff in life, around a bend, down a rabbit hole.

As the bus slips through alternating patches of shadow and sunlight along the road, the hum of the wheels on asphalt lulls him into a stupor that's not quite sleep. He leans his head against the bus window and remembers similar mornings on dissimilar journeys with the radio playing and the girl in the passenger seat of her car. Over dinner, he told her he's leaving. She doesn't react. It's remote to her, another world she doesn't know or understand. But her body sends an electric current through his; all that matters is the moment. The fragrance of sun-warmed skin and honeysuckle, hair and flesh soft to the touch.

He starts out of his reverie when the driver downshifts and the Greyhound bus jolts to a stop in another bus station to pick up more inductees. This group fills the remaining seats, and he finds himself crowded against the window by a heavy-set draftee with impressive body odor and a nervous tic that makes his chin bob up and down.

The bus leaves the city street and moves onto a highway. He and his seatmate exchange names and quickly exhaust their common topics of interest. Around them, muted conversations continue among the ones who know each other, but their voices soon merge with the clack of the wheels on rough pavement. He leans his head back against the window, now warmed by the sun, and drifts away again, seeing her in front of the mirror, brushing her hair, admiring her reflection. He walks up behind her, puts his arms around her waist, his bare chest against her warm back, and stares over her shoulder into the mirror.

The bus pulls into a gravel parking area next to a concrete building, an abandoned service station, stopping beneath a blue-and-white Greyhound sign sticking out from one corner. Six more future warriors come on board. Most wear blue jeans and thin jackets, except for one with mod-striped pants. All but two of them have long sideburns and non-descript, swept-back hair or Beatles haircuts. The lone black inductee sits down in the first seat by himself. A large, stocky boy with a retro-crew cut, round red cheeks, and neatly pressed blue jeans goes to the bench seat in the back. Nobody says anything.

He again rouses with a start as the bus stops. The sun slants at an angle through the window, and he shades his eyes to watch a Military Policeman talking to the bus driver and then waving the bus through the gate. They have arrived.

They are issued fatigues and underwear, combat boots, plastic helmet liner, steel pot, and poncho; told to change and stuff the rest of their new gear into a duffel bag. They receive boxes to ship their civilian clothes and other artifacts home—all of it, including paperback books and school rings. His Carolina ring, he'll never wear again. The bus stops a last time in front of a row of faded-yellow wooden barracks on a low knoll, within an expanse of sandy soil and red dirt. A single tall pine stands next to the corner of one building.

A sergeant in pressed khakis, a Smoky-the-bear hat slanted down over his eyes, gets on the bus and stalks down the aisle and back. The inductees look expectantly at him while he stares down the rows of seats.

"All right, you long-haired, pansy-ass faggots, your sorry asses are mine for the next eight weeks." The brim of his hat sweeps slowly back and forth over their upturned faces. "You - are - trainees. And I - am - god." He pauses. "You are the lowest pieces of shit on this fucking earth, lower than a snake's belly, more worthless than worm shit." He grins, his eyes obscured by the Smoky hat. "You *will* address me as 'Drill Sergeant,' and I will address you as 'trainee.' You *will* give me affirmative and negative answers when I ask you a question." He pauses, then shouts, "Is—that—understood?"

Low mumbles come from some among the eclectic mix of young men on the bus, nothing but silence from a few, including the ex-grad student, and a loud "yes sir" from the back of the bus—the stocky inductee with the retro crew cut.

"What a sorry-ass bunch of limp-dick faggots. You're nothing but no-good ass-wipes—all of you. When I ask you something, sound off like you got a pair of balls between your legs instead of a greasy cunt. Do you understand me?" This time he shouts in a voice that seems to shake the bus.

"Yes, Drill Sergeant!" almost all, including the ex-grad student, shout back. Crew cut's "Yes sir, Drill Sergeant" stands out.

His eyes fixed on crew cut, the drill sergeant strides to the back of the bus and stares down at the boy, no more than eighteen, while everyone else turns to watch. "You do *not* call me 'sir,' faggot. That's for ass-wipe officers."

The heel of a polished jump boot comes down on crew cut's foot and the great khaki god pivots on the other toe. Crew cut cries out in pain, and the ex-grad student can see his lower lip quivering.

The drill sergeant remains poised for a moment in crew cut's face, then walks back to the front of the bus. He turns and speaks softly. "For the next eight weeks, I am your mother, your father, your girlfriend, your fucking priest. You got nobody here to go crying to but me. And you ain't dog shit until I finish with you." His voice rises. "You don't eat, sleep, shit, piss, or do anything else . . . unless I tell you." His voice drops on the last phrase and the bus is silent. He waits, staring along each row. "Is that understood?" he yells.

"Yes, Drill Sergeant."

"I—can't—hear—you."

"Yes, Drill Sergeant!" they yell louder.

"Are you a bunch of fucking pansies?"

"No, Drill Sergeant!" they roar at the top of their lungs.

"That's better, ladies. You sweet peas hav-ta make up your minds about how you wanta come outta here. Most of you bunch of pussies are going to Nam." He pauses. "Where you'll meet ol' Charlie Cong. He's going to try to kill your ugly ass." He stops. "I been there." The hat sweeps across their faces, some frightened, some blank, a few eager. "Been there twice. And come back." Another pause. "I'm here to show you how it's done . . . If you listen, you might learn something. You might just make it back on two legs." He looks around again, his eyes black darts under the smoky hat. "If you don't listen, Uncle Sam's got plenty of body bags to go around."

And so the new life begins. "O lost and by the wind grieved."*

What has he lost?

---

* Thomas Wolfe, *Look Homeward Angel*

Freedom, dignity, humanity.

The next morning, a drill instructor marches them first to the barbershop to have their heads shorn and then to the dentist for an inventory of teeth, leaving them standing in the 95-degree heat while each makes a visit inside. Sweat runs down the ex-grad student's neck, his back, and over his forehead and into his eyes—glasses sliding down his nose, head pounding in the sun. Then the instructor marches them to the Mess Hall, calling cadences, "Jody's got your girl and gone, sound off, one, two . . ." and makes them do two trips through the parallel bars before chow. Those who fall off, like the ex-grad student, do pushups and bring up the end of the chow line so that they have only a few minutes to eat before the drill sergeants stomp through the Mess Hall and sweep the trays off the tables and onto the floor, to be cleaned up by the unlucky ones on KP.

Back in the barracks area, all three platoons in the training company are ordered to "fall in" for a welcoming speech by the company commander. The drill sergeant for the ex-grad student's platoon, Sergeant Deakins, has arrived. He stalks back and forth, a predator watching its prey, as the skinhead trainees form ranks with a great deal of shuffling and stumbling. Drill Sergeant Deakins towers over the front row of trainees like a huge black grizzly bear. His head is so big that the Smoky-the-bear hat, pulled down over his eyes, covers only the front half of his head. A scowl creases his face as he glowers at his new charges.

The ex-grad student rushes to the middle of the fourth rank, following his instincts to become inconspicuous, anonymous. In front, he sees his bus seatmate, Aaron Sprinkle, stumble into the first row next to a skinny black kid, a high school dropout named Freddy Cline. While they wait, standing at attention, Cline, who has already demonstrated a penchant for volubility, says something to Sprinkle in a loud whisper that can be heard from three rows back.

"What'd ya say, boy?" Sergeant Deakins shrieks and lumbers over to Cline from his line of march in front of the ranks. For such a huge man, Deakins' voice is high-pitched and shrill. "Ya got somethin' to say in my platoon, ya say it to me. What'd ya say, ya scrawny little cocksucker?"

"Nothing, Drill Sergeant!" Cline yells. He *is* scrawny, and short, but he can sound off in a loud voice, even if it is a bit squeaky.

Deakins shifts to Sprinkle. "Ya quaeer or somethin'? Gotta whisper to each other in my fuckin' formation?"

Sprinkle's nervous tic starts, and Deakins moves closer, his big head bent down inches away from Sprinkle's face. The longer Deakins stares, the more Sprinkle's head jumps up and down, neck scrunching up as the chin juts forward, the sweat popping out on the back of his neck.

"Hey, Smith, ya see this?" Deakins yells over his shoulder. "Come heah and watch this fucker's head go." Drill Sergeant Smith, the white sergeant who greeted them on the bus, strides over, hands on hips, and stands beside Deakins, maliciously grinning at Sprinkle's malaise.

"What your name, shaky?" Deakins asks in a voice loud enough for the entire platoon to hear. Sprinkle starts to give a stuttering answer, but Deakins cuts him off. "It don't matter what your fuckin' mamma called ya. From now on, ya gonna be called 'Shaky' in my platoon, and you better goddamn well answer when I call ya, ya understand me?"

Sprinkle's head continues its up-and-down motion, and large welts start appearing on the back of his neck above his sweat-stained fatigue collar. The ex-grad student seethes at the young trainee's humiliation—and fears that Deakins will notice him next.

Sprinkle doesn't answer.

"I said, do ya understand me, ya fuckin' faggot," Deakins yells. Drill Sergeant Smith is laughing out loud now, slapping his thigh in glee.

"Ye-ye-yes, D-Drill S-Sergeant," Sprinkle finally gets out.

Deakins steps back in front of Cline and stands looking at him. "Ya think it's funny? I don't want no butt-fucking nigger qua-eers in my platoon, ya understand, boy?"

"I'm not queer, Drill Sergeant," Cline says in a strained voice, not as loud as before. The muscles in Cline's neck grow taut.

Deakins reaches out a huge paw and grabs Cline by the collar of his shirt. "I didn't askt ya what ya were, boy. I askt ya if ya understood me."

He pulls Cline's face close to his so that Cline is up on his toes. Deakins glances over at Sprinkle and grins. Sprinkle's tic has hit overdrive and red hives cover his neck. Deakins reaches out with his free hand and grabs the collar of Sprinkle's shirt; then in one quick motion, he pops the heads of the two trainees together with a "thunk" audible even in the back row. Deakins pushes the two away from him, and they stumble into the trainees in the ranks behind them. Their caps askew, the two recover their places, Cline visibly trembling, Sprinkle with his vicious tic. Neither gives any cry of pain.

"Line those troops up," a grizzled black soldier with the stripes of a First Sergeant shouts as he comes striding in front of the ranks. He has a rugged face that would be handsome except for a livid scar that stretches from the right side of his square jaw to the edge of his right eye. His voice comes out as a deep, no-nonsense baritone, and he glares at the two drill sergeants, who have backed away from Cline and Sprinkle and stand laughing at the terror they have inflicted on their subjects.

"Atten-shun," the First Sergeant yells, and a gaunt, pallidly white First Lieutenant wearing jump boots and black rim glasses vaults onto a platform in front of the new trainees. They come to attention, and the Lieutenant looks them over.

"At ease, men," he bellows, his voice echoing off the wooden walls of the barracks behind the ranks of trainees.

He pauses while they relax from their stiff postures. "Welcome - to - Fort Bragg - and army - basic training," he barks in clipped phrases. He smacks a swagger stick against one leg and gives a tight-lipped smile as he surveys his troops, General Patton before his army. "Everyone happy - with your - accommodations - here in - B Company?" he shouts.

A faint "yes sir" ripples through the ranks.

The First Sergeant leaps onto the platform. "The Lieutenant asked if you're happy with your new home," he yells in his baritone voice, his chin jutting out. "Let's show some respect here and sound off, like - you - got - a - pair."

"Yes sir!" they all shout in unison. The noise reverberates and echoes off the ancient wooden barracks behind them and over the podium in front.

Basic Training—some images linger and seep out from the walls of the mind. Sitting in front of a desk, giving "personal data" to a civilian clerk-typist—knowing it's for graves registration—and listening to the heavy trucks rumble by under the open windows, trying to stay awake, staring at the late morning sun on the trees across the street. Then focusing on the shaved-head trainee at the next desk, something familiar about him—the square face and red complexion—recognition and exclamation. At the University, a student committee of some sort. A fellow sufferer, drafted, finished his first year of law school only by the grace of the local draft board. And here he is, caught in the same web of absurdity.

Learning to march—go to your left, your right, your left. Sound off!—one, two, three, four. Private Floyd, a pigeon-toed, ebony draftee who grins at everything, bounces and sways, almost dancing, swinging his arms like this is grand fun. His legs dissolve into the future, and he comes home in a wheelchair, so says the friend who saw him again, back at Fort Bragg. Does Private Floyd win a medal?

Falling out after taps to stand at attention in white T-shirts and boxer shorts—"right shoulder footlockers!" Low crawling around the barracks in their underwear at midnight in the misting rain and mud. Private Jakes crawling under the barracks and going to sleep, and everyone looking for him.

Private Jakes standing at attention in front of the barracks with his rifle and pack.

Private Sprinkle, a.k.a. Shaky, at the firing range, shooting at the 100-meter target and his M-14 rifle comes apart, pieces flying through the air—no one hurt . . . this time. Private Sprinkle standing at attention in front of the barracks—alone, for hours. Drill Sergeant Deakins in his face, yelling, "Y're quaeer, ain't ya boy? Answer me!" Grabbing Private Sprinkle's M-14 and bringing the butt down on Sprinkle's foot. Sprinkle's head bobbing up and down. "Don't ya ever fuck up a rifle like that again," the huge grizzly bear roars, "or I'll personally stomp yo ugly ass into the ground."

Throwing hand grenades—pull the pin, pop the lever, count, throw, and duck below the bunker wall. Private Cline inside one concrete bunker with Sergeant Deakins; the rest of the platoon lined up on the berm behind the line of bunkers, waiting their turn, listening to the grenade bursts in the sandbagged area beyond the bunkers. Deakins barking instructions and everyone waiting on Cline to throw his grenade. And waiting. Then a yell, curses, and Cline flying over the back wall of the bunker—suspended at the end of Deakins' giant arms, and Deakins coming over behind him just before a loud, echoing explosion erupts from inside.

Private Cline standing in front of the barracks at attention for hours, Deakins sitting in a chair, glaring at him.

Formation before chow: "Order arms!" Stand and wait, and wait. "Ground arms." Everyone places his pack and rifle on the ground. "Fall out!" Everyone rushes to the barracks. Except Jakes, who remains standing, rifle at order arms by his side, head down—alone amid the four rows of packs and M-14s. Asleep, just Jakes and the lone pine tree standing by the barracks.

KP for twelve hours. On the back sink, washing pots and pans, white T-shirt wet with sweat and grease, fatigues soaked and stained with greasy water, and Jakes standing with his hands in the hot suds, holding a pan, not moving.

"Get your dumb ass out of my kitchen, you lazy fucking nigger," yells the cook.

Private Jakes at a table folding paper napkins, holding one in midair in front of a dispenser, elbows on the table . . . asleep. Narcolepsy? Master of deception? Medical Discharge? Blown to bits in Nam? To sleep, perchance to dream.

Some images never fade.

Drill Sergeant Deakins, after a night in town, coming through the barracks at 2:00am, kicking foot lockers into the side aisle, throwing a metal trash can onto the polished floor, picking up boots and flinging them left and right into the double bunks and metal wall lockers, barking curses and threats at anyone not out of his bunk and outside in two minutes.

In the mornings, when the overhead lights come on at 4:00am, pitch dark outside, the sound of dog tags rattling up and down the barracks as bare feet thud onto wooden floors and wall lockers clang open and shut. Air redolent of Lysol and floor wax.

Airborne troops running down the dark street chant as they run:

I wanta be an Airborne Ranger,

I wanta live a life of danger,

I wanta go to Vi-etnam,

I wanta kill ol' Charlie Cong.

Airborne! All the way!

Deakins saying the only thing that falls out of the sky is bird shit and fools.

A hot July night. They gather around a small black-and-white television screen, the set hooked to a cord through the window of the Mess Hall. The Eagle has landed. "Hey, you! You got fireguard. Hell no, you can't wait for him to go down the fucking ladder. Get your ass up there and relieve Jakes. Sorry shit's probably already asleep."

Only later does he hear, "One small step for a man, one giant leap for mankind."

Vietnam waiting just over the horizon, waiting to be fed.

After five weeks of torture, a Sunday morning finally brings visitors for the inmates. Barracks and latrines sparkle, windows glint in the sun. Hard red dirt and sand raked clean in even lines, no cigarette butts anywhere.

Dress Khaki's, cunt caps, so called by the drill sergeants, perched square on shaved heads. Waiting in the hot summer North Carolina coastal tidelands sun. Land of tobacco and cotton, rebel flags and old slave markets. Fort Bragg: a military base surrounded by pine trees, scrub oaks, sand hills, and golf courses. Named after a Confederate general, a rebel, a traitor.

The ex-grad student's mother, aunt, and uncle arrive in the uncle's new air-conditioned Pontiac. Two strong-willed, unschooled, country-raised sisters, so loyal they still fight like siblings after sixty years. They bring cold fried chicken, biscuits, deviled eggs, sweet iced tea, and devils-food cake, his favorite. The four of them eat at a wooden table in a picnic area near the parade grounds, under loblolly and long-leaf pines, his freshly shined, black dress shoes scuffed by the sand.

Another training company parades by in their dress Khaki's, preparing for graduation, rifles on shoulders, flags flying, moving smoothly in unison as a single unit to the drill sergeant's cadence calls—sanitized, nothing about Jody and what he's doing to your girl while your girl and your mother may be listening.

Uncle, watching the martial display, bursting with pride at being an American, fascinated by the pageantry, the beauty of men marching, the resonant voice of the drill sergeant—go to your left, your right, your left—and the booming response of the men as they go by, then wheel left to the other side of the field, each rank turning seamlessly at the corner. And the ghosts marching among them, in tri-cornered hats with muskets, dark blue uniforms with brass buttons and gray with rag-bound feet, all carrying long rifles mounted with bayonets, men in spats and bloused trousers, men in fatigues still stained with the mud of French fields, row after row after row after row, the Arc de Triomphe looming behind them. The uncle, not a veteran, observing what a stirring sight the solid ranks of soldiers make, this powerful, singular mass of men in motion as one—how exciting this must be. Not seeing the rows of white crosses and stars of David and flat tombstones turning green with moss rank on rank on rank across the rolling turf.

Vietnam waiting around the corner—go to your left, your right, your left—waiting with open arms to receive its tribute.

The newly minted Private First Class, the only identity he has now, gazes out of an airplane window for the first time, marveling at the white clouds through which they are passing, at the neat rows of houses below and the bare December trees around them. In the distance are tall buildings framed by the gray mass of Stone Mountain and the memorial to Confederate icons and the Ku Klux Klan. He is only one of the thousands of soldiers—a mélange of races and backgrounds—moving across America like lines of ants to converge on San Francisco, three time zones west. Leaving their home soil the next day, most for the first time, they will not see the tinsel decorations and Christmas lights go up along the main streets, and they will not follow the countdown of shopping days, more important to those back home—those not affected—than the body count from the far-away war.

One plane load after another leaves Travis Air Base, their live cargo outfitted with new green jungle fatigues, jungle boots, and olive drab underwear. The safe and cheery commercial airlines, flying the friendly skies, profit from ferrying troops to South Vietnam, replenishing the hordes of American soldiers already there and recycling the spent forces home, back to "the real world." Clean and pleasant Pan Am jets, their seats more modern and comfortable than the furniture many leave behind in their small homes, bear them up into the night sky. Over the Pacific, pretty young women in blue uniforms bring orange juice to callow soldiers, most not yet old enough to vote, in this era, for or against either the war or those who have dispatched them to fight it.

The only remarkable aspect of this ages-old phenomenon—only the names, dates, and places changed from times past—is how the not-so-randomly-selected few go to war like sheep while their luckier or smarter or shrewder or wealthier brethren stay home. Cheering them on. Thanking whatever gods may be that they are not going too. They have better things to do, they think and say only later, much later. Only the insane or the brave or the foolish or the patriotic or the hapless few, willingly or unwillingly, go to war.

Or perhaps this is not so remarkable, not so different from before. Or after.

The plane lands at Bien Hoa Air Base near Saigon before dawn, and the new reality, or unreality, begins. How will it end? Some will go home as cargo on these same jets, the pretty young women treading the cabin floor above them.

He steps off the plane in the dark, walks down the ramp onto the tarmac, just like in Atlanta, but immediately the heat, the humidity, the rumble of noise, and the smell hit him. Especially the heat and the smell, like walking through a garbage dump. No—different. Something decaying and putrid and burning, like rags or flesh, a smell of ancient loam fused with lime, mold, feces, and diesel fumes.

As the military bus roars through the narrow streets of the waking village, they see and hear and smell Vietnam like they will see and hear and smell it forever. It rises up before them through dirty, wire-covered glass in the pre-dawn gloom: shadowy figures riding on scooters, in three-wheel Lambrettas or military trucks; people trudging along the road, scrambling out of the way as the bus careens past them; dogs running and barking by the wheels; chickens flying out of the street, into doorways. They are entering a tunnel into another world, another time. "Yea though I walk through the valley . . ." The bus leaves the village and turns onto a dark highway between rice paddies that extend far into the gloom.

The bus disgorges them at an assembly area in Long Binh to await in-country processing and assignment to their units. Sitting together on a small hill, they watch the sun rise on them for the first time in this place. The growing light reveals a perimeter fence and guard bunkers down the hill, and beyond the perimeter, a stretch of bare red dirt dotted with almost leafless shrubs leading up a slope to a highway in the distance. Trucks spewing black smoke, jeeps, motor scooters, even a few automobiles speed back and forth, silhouetted against the brightening sky. The sun comes up over the highway—a dull red orb in a yellow haze—and the sky above turns pastel blue with wisps of pink clouds. At home, it is twilight, the day before. He looks around at the others clustered on the hill, some dozing or pretending to doze, some like him, watching, trying to see this new land, to understand what it is, what lies in front of them. They will be here, under this strange sun, in this unreal place as different from home as night from day, a year, 365 dawns, one at a time, hour by hour. If they make it, they will have to find their way back through the tunnel at some other dawn.

Murray Moseley sits across the aisle in study hall. Quiet, dark eyebrows, not a scholar—a ladies' man and football team co-captain who hums to himself and smiles like the

Mona Lisa when he strolls back from the pencil sharpener. No college for him. Murray Moseley goes to war. Patriotism— God, flag, and country. Gung ho. Hits the beach in '66. Dead in weeks.

Lieutenant Elwood Greene. The ex-grad student knew him in college as Elwood, the kid who always had a goofy grin, struggled to make B's and C's, lived behind the door across the hall in the dorm. At least that's the memory. Rumor has it he went to Officers Candidate School and came out a lieutenant, and a jerk. Eight weeks or so into his tour in Nam, he walks into a village, comes out on a Medevac, in a body bag. Where did the grenade come from?

And the list goes on.

More than 58,000 Americans dead, their names etched on a black wall set amid a sacrilege of politicos who cry the havoc of patriotism, but never make the sacrifice. And countless men with missing legs or arms or fucked-up minds.

How many Vietnamese dead? Two million Cambodians? And all the maimed.

And what was it all for? What we learn, we soon forget.

The wound does not heal because the metaphor is wrong.

Vietnam, the war: one more event in the flow of human history, worse than some of the more benign catastrophes, but not even close to many others. The Vietnam War, to the Americans, remains significant only for those who survive it and come to view it through the prism of their own experience. The American War in the People's Republic of Vietnam.

For the dead Americans, Vietnam is no longer significant.

As to the Vietnam veterans, they should be neither seen nor heard, or so they are told. Just go away. Don't remind us. America's failure. The great mistake. Oops.

Only the words and the pictures keep the events from fading with the deaths of those who survive. The archived film footage tells a story that is dumbly watched and not understood.

Is history always forgotten? Denied? Repeated?

Words. Strung together in different ways by different people, distilled through the kaleidoscope of different experiences, needs, and desires.

Words.

What do they mean?

PAGE SIXTEEN

... I Remember The People; Now, Will They Survive?

By Jim Garrison
St. Dunstan's, Houston

I recall the December morning I landed at Bein Hoa air base near Saigon. At 4 a.m., it was hot and muggy, quite a contrast to the crisp fall air I had left in the States. From the military bus careening through narrow streets before dawn, I caught my first glimpse of the people and their culture. In the dim light, I saw men, women and children in strange, pointed hats and dark, pajama-like clothes, on bicycles and walking, darting out of the way of the bus. There were soldiers in bunkers surrounded by constantina wire. Later I discovered that whole families might be living in such bunkers. For the first, time I smelled strange incense and foods cooking and I heard the racket of the xich-loc and the sing-song cadence of Vietnamese.

Ten years later, I met a refugee couple from this same part of the world where I had marked each of 386 days on a calendar in hopes of going home. The couple was from Laos and they had left their home forever. Their entire life's possessions consisted of two or three boxes and a couple of plastic bags plus some furniture, clothes, food and other items the congregation of St. Dunstan's Episcopal Church had given them.

My situation ten years before does not compare well with what this couple is experiencing. But the same fear of what will happen must be there. And the overriding question must inevitably arise: "Will we survive?" I'm sure they will, but only with help.

St. Dunstan's Refugee Resettlement Committee was formed by some of the congregation between August and November 1979, primarily as a result of the now waning publicity given to the plight of the boat people escaping Vietnam. From the inquiries we made came an understanding that, as to the total problem of the boat people, very little could be done. However, we could help those Indochinese refugees who had already escaped the oppressive governments and conditions in that area and had come to this country. Various groups and organizations had formed sponsorship programs to help meld these diverse people into our society by finding jobs and housing and educating them to a new culture.

The first family sponsored by the committee was the Phasavaths, husband

Refugees and members of St. Dunstan's take a "moving" break and enjoy American sandwiches during a recent bout of resettling for the parish's new family.

Khomone and wife Bouaveng, who had been living in the YMCA Welcome Center at Missouri City for about a month since their arrival in the U.S. Bouaveng and Khamone had come from a camp in Thailand after escaping from Laos. Khamone and some friends swam across the Mekong River more than four years ago. Bouaveng followed her husband only within the past year. A four-year-old daughter is still in Laos with her grandparents.

Khamone began work January 2 at a job obtained through a member of the congregation. He and his wife had moved to an apartment near his job December 23. It had been furnished through donations with food, clothing and basic household items. Since then, committee members have frequently visited the Phasavaths to give them moral support and to help them adjust to our culture. Bank accounts, garbage disposals, electrical appliances, shopping, transportation (or lack of it), thermostats, new foods, clock radios and beds are just a few of the strange new things they have had to cope with.

One of the biggest adjustments for them, however, has been learning to live alone. The Phasavaths come from a culture based upon the extended family and Khomone and Bouaveng are isolated without family and friends living with them. This is even more frustrating for Bouaveng who is pregnant and she must face having her baby in an impersonal American hospital rather than in the Laotian manner, at home with her family performing traditional rituals associated with childbirth,

To help ease the culture shock experienced by the first family, our committee chose to resettle nearby, as quickly as possible, friends of the Phasavaths, Khoxayo Buonkong, his wife and their six children. The congregation is currently painting, repairing and furnishing a rental house so that the Khoxayos can move in soon. The families, together, can help each other cope with the cultural transition in a manner that we could not hope to to accomplish by ourselves.

Meeting these families and seeing their situation, jogs my memory of my first morning on Vietnamese soil, watching the sunrise on a vacant field of brown dirt, the constantina wire, and the highway that led to Saigon and wondering what would come next. I also remember the people, especially the children, I met there, and I hope that what will come next for them, and for those who escape, will not be more suffering.

I recall the December morning I landed at Bien Hoa air base near Saigon. At 4 a.m., it was hot and muggy, quite a contrast to the crisp fall air I had left in the States. From the military bus careening through narrow streets before dawn, I caught my first glimpse of the people and their culture. In the dim light, I saw men, women and children in strange, pointed hats and [dark], pajama-like clothes, on bicycles and walking, darting out of the way of the bus. There were soldiers in bunkers surrounded by [concertina] wire. Later I discovered that whole families might be living in such bunkers. For the first time I smelled strange incense and foods cooking and I heard the racket of the [xich-lo's] and the sing-song cadence of Vietnamese.

Ten years later, I met a refugee couple from the same part of the world where I had marked each of 386 days on a calendar in hopes of going home. The couple was from Laos and they had left their home forever. Their entire life's possessions consisted of two or three boxes and a couple of plastic bags plus some furniture, clothes, food and other items the congregation of St. Dunstan's Episcopal Church had given them.

My situation ten years before does not compare well with what this couple is experiencing. But the same fear of what will happen must be there. And the overriding question must inevitably arise: "Will we survive?" I'm sure they will, but only with help.

STORIES AND ESSAYS
NOTES AND PUBLICATION INDEX

Fiction:

1. **The Outpost**: Three soldiers and a native girl are the only ones remaining in a remote aerie overlooking the desert, where the soldiers have been left to signal if the enemy is pursuing the retreating army to the capital. While this story mirrors the French-Algerian war of the 1950s, it could be set in any number of different places and times. The first draft was written in 2004-05. [Published by *The Book Smugglers Den*, Issue 12, March 2020]

2. **Fat Juliet**: A young lawyer tries to save a baby bird while she, in turn, needs saving from a criminal client trying to force her to reveal the name of a confidential informant. The unlikely rescuer is her cat, Fat Juliet, serving as the intermediary for an alien on the planet A'Onia.

3. **Break the Bubble**: A whistle-blower confronts a dystopian world where the wealthiest have the ultimate in health protection and everyone else dies young. The first draft was written long before the Covid pandemic of 2020-2022. The story was inspired by an earlier virus scare in 2012 and the debate over affordable health care in the United States, along with the

growing disparities in wealth between rich and poor worldwide.

4. **Across the Divide**: A soldier on an overnight pass hitchhikes hundreds of miles over Carolina back roads to find his Dulcinea. Instead, he encounters a cast of characters who illustrate how much more than distance separate people. [Published by *Wraparound South*, Spring 2020 online issue]

5. **Mick**: A soldier of principle and strong beliefs is confronted by a top sergeant, intoxicated and unprincipled, as seen through lens tinted by Kafka. [Published in *Untold Stories, An Anthology*, Military Writers Society of America 2021]

Creative nonfiction and essays:

6. **Why I Write (or the house my father built)** [Published in *Reading Nation Magazine*, June 2021]

7. **Strangers on the Appalachian Trail**: walking on the trail with a lost young man. [Published in *The Moving Force Journal*, Fall/Winter 2020 (issue 3)]

8. **The Poisoning**: Based on a coroner's inquest into the suspicious death by poisoning of a white family patriarch, one of the author's ancestors, in Post-Reconstruction North Carolina. A "small black boy" who stayed with the family was suspected. [Published in *Works in Progress Anthology*, Three Dogs Write Press, December 2021]

9. **Time to Go**: For a ninety-year-old woman confined to a wheelchair in an assisted living facility, it isn't time to die, just time to get out of this repulsive place full of

old people. [Published by *daCunha Nonfiction*, daCunha. global online, April 2017]

10. **Looking for Gary Cheers**: You never know when the last time will be you'll ever see someone, a friend or former lover, not family, but someone you intend to call or go see just to find out how they're doing. But it's too late. [Published by *Manhattanville Review*, Fall 2017]

11. **Vietnam Story (A Draftee's Lament)**: Memories of the Vietnam War era after 50 years.

POETRY

I AM NOT A POET

I am not a poet.
I do not write poetry.
I do not write poems about writing poetry.
I record impressions, images, ideas, conundrums,
     if not from the heart, from the amygdala.
When I was a lawyer,
I followed three rules for practicing law:
     never assume anything;
     never trust anybody;
     consistency is the hobgoblin of little minds;
     no generalization is worth a damn.
The first came from experience;
     the second from a high school English teacher
     (and a hundred pages of tightly written notes).
The rest?
From Emerson and Holmes (Oliver not Sherlock)
     by way of Justice Hugo Black, in part,
     bastardized and personalized.
In the beginning,
     at the end,
     they still apply.
Life is a puzzle,
     the universe a mystery.
     (Or is it universes?)
But I am not a lawyer—
     and I am not a poet.

WHY DID HEMINGWAY KILL HIMSELF?

We're all going skiing today.
We adults are apprehensive,
        not sure of how our old bodies will react.
I stand on the porch with my coffee and gaze out:
        the lake is a shimmery blue;
        the mountains, almost black, divide the lake
        from the blue sky.
The wet bark and boughs of the pines near the cabin
        frame the lake, mountains, and sky—
        on the mountains white patches of snow.

Why did Hemingway kill himself when he wasn't
        dying?
What did he wake and see in the mirror one morning?
What was he afraid of?
Was it death?
He feared death so much that he ran into her arms,
        to escape the fear?
Was it the weakening of his body?
A debilitating, wasting disease?
Disgust at what he had become?
He lived in a cabin, in a wild and pristine place.
Was it not enough to look out across the forest,
        hear the birds, see the mountains against the
        sky?
To squeeze out of life one last breath of cold air,

the light refracted through the trees,
the red and yellow flowers in the meadow,
the blue sky,
and process it all through rods and cones,
sparking billions of stars in his sentient self?
Different from trees that stand mute, mindless,
unseeing.

Why did Hemingway kill himself
when perhaps he could write one more
paragraph,
one more sentence
that described simply and directly
the world, life,
even if no one would publish it or ever read it?

THE WENCH IS DEAD

(with apologies to Christopher Marlowe)

It was a troubled time,
fraught with turmoil
and war in a foreign land,
a time long past,
so why should I care now?

A brief meeting of bodies,
nothing more than flesh pressed close,
lips and tongues touching,
breaths commingled,
laughter, sighs, and cries;
a matador twirling a bright red cape,
teasing a russet bull
pulling the room around.
But why remember all that now?

Translucent oil, white skin, white sheets,
head thrown back, a pulsing vein,
honeysuckle scent on a sun-warmed neck;
a new dawn's light windshield reflected,
green spring leaves flashing by,
sun-yellowed in a fine new morning.
Why should I care still?

Lips, fingers, breath,
long past, long gone;
passion, sunlight, voice,
faded and dead,
never to engage the senses again.
All that remains are floating remnants
of a struggling memory,
lingering, tugging at the synapses—
and those, too, shall die.
So why should I care even now?

VINH LONG AT DUSK

A fading memory
      imbued with yellow
superimposed on white stucco buildings
      and red tile roofs,
yellow dusk reverberating with the staccato
      celebration of
      Japanese and Italian labor,
echoing in a cacophony of horns and voices
      choked with exhaust fumes.

No trees,
concrete streets, broken sidewalks,
a water-filled gutter
      with a crying, bare-assed child squatting on a plank
      leading to the bar with the bright blue gate
under a sky suffused with yellow,
      lost in yellow,
      swallowed in yellow,
in the deceptive
      somnambulant grip
      of the tropical twilight,
a hiatus between the human clamor of day
and the artillery rung, fog-seized silence of night.

THE RUNNER

I walk
when I should run,
thinking there is time
when there is none.

I run
when I should walk
and take
the time to talk.

I think
that I am late,
when there
is
always
. . .
time
. . .
to
. . .
wait.

WHITE GUILT

I suffer from white guilt.
Not that I ever did anything to anyone or
      that any of my direct ancestors did:
      yeoman farmers, craftsmen,
      wives birthing until they died or shriveled up,
      living off the land, tilling the soil,
      cutting the trees, planing the wood.

But maybe they did,
      owned slaves, sold babies, separated families.
Or maybe there was only the acquiescence of
      acceptance,
      the support for suppression of others
      not of their tribe.
Maybe they were only ordinary Germans,
      unknowing of the death camps
      but aware of deportations,
      of the vitriol and hatred,
      of breaking glass and burning books,
      of people no longer there.

How do you expiate a collective sin?
Not by burying it, forgetting it,
denying it,
flying the flag of oppression.

When those who committed the sins are gone
    and those who suffered are dead
    and only the DNA, the blood, continues,
    does the sin continue
    from generation unto generation?

I think not.
Each generation has its own sins,
    each individual his own culpability,
    bred from what came before
    and embraced
    and nurtured
    and savored
    as her own.

ON GROWING OLD AND DISCOVERING TRUTH

My days are measured
By bottles of discount wine,
My weeks by clean linens;
Each morning
I seek salvation
      in a cafe benison.

Sleep, sleep divine,
Why should eternal sleep
      not be heaven?

For religion begins
Where knowledge ends.

My little fame in life,
      I know,
Will be confined
      to a freeway sign:
           "Missing Elderly,"
           numinous against
           a gray morning sky,
Flashing, flashing, flashing
      above a highway exit.

The door was closed
    and did not open,
So how did the cat
    go out again?
But remembering to floss
    gives each day
    a bright new meaning.

So knowledge ends
Where religion begins.

Italy's third volcano,
    what's it called?
Not Etna or Vesuvius,
The one in the movie we saw?
I forget, though I should know;
And not Olympus,
    with Hera and Zeus
    and Jove.

For us mortals, what does it signify
    when we purchase stain remover
      by the gallon?
Pessimism of drooled spaghetti
    or long life's delusive,
      grand ambition?

All hail *Staphylococcus*,
    with my name on it;
Where fear reigns,
    religion gains.

Dough, the financial guru says,
    you'll need 'til you're ninety-five,
      or perhaps, I think,
        to .38,
Or maybe I'll rob a bank
    or fail to pay my taxes
      for a prison bunk
      and hospital bed.
But what about the poor teller,
    the cop
    and the unlucky feller
who has to clean up the mess?

But hark!
The coffee grinder churns,
    the espresso machine
      still renders,
    so why should I surrender?

Yea, verily, I declare
    on my life's embers
where true knowledge ends
    unyielding ignorance begins
      and religion wins.

WE WERE IN THE WATER THEN

We dive and clasp
Legs and arms entangled like seaweed
Touching
      pressing
      rubbing
In a womb of water
      the deep end of the pool
      below the diving boards
Your sliding flesh under my hands
Your hands clasping my arms
Twisting away
      slipping
           out of my grasp
In liquid embrace that's only play
Beneath the blue surface
Hair twirling about your face
And wrapping around my neck
Each other's bodies
Long and slender in youth
Of we two swimmers
Red trunks against black-and-white striped bikini
Rough under my fingers as I grab your naked waist
And you twist away and up
And we break the surface
     you first then me
Sputtering

    laughing
You throw back your head
And fling out your hair
Before you dive again and I come after you
Down,
     down,
        down
             to the cement bottom
Grabbing your leg above the knee
Pulling myself along your body
Sliding up
    and you back to me
Until we come together
Entwined again
Legs and arms and heads
Almost as one
We roll and spin
Up and up
    into the light
Breaking the surface
Gasping for air
A geyser of flesh
Oblivious to those
    who watch from sterile land
Our sexual encounter
Without consummation
Or conclusion.

IN THE END?

What will get us in the end?
Will it be the wages
      of original sin?
Or something
      we've done
          just for fun
Like our long hours
      in the sun?
Or some deadly disease:
      a super coronavirus
      or a meta-staphylococcus?

What will get us in the end?
Is it just around the bend?
Or over a distant hill,
In the shape of a little pill?
Or will it be
      our own
          private hell
Poured out of a bottle,
      at full throttle?

Or stress from overwork?
All those extra slabs of pork?
The hand of an angry God?
Or the insane ravings
      of an ur-religious sod?

This I know for sure,
Our demise
    will certainly inure
To the good of mankind
And the child
    who's left behind
That we
    who've had our day
Get the hell
    out of the way.

WAR'S CHILD

"Look homeward Angel now, and melt with ruth,
And O ye *Dolphins*, waft the hapless youth.
        Weep no more, woeful shepherds weep no more,
For Lycidas your sorrow is not dead,
Sunk though he be beneath the wat'ry floor . . ."
        (From "Lycidas" by John Milton.)

We all knew her—
the army and I—
we called her Syphilitic Sandy:
war's sister, mother, and child,
a fusion of east and west,
bred by the last
conquering horde,
lusted for by the next.
A dark angel of desire,
soaring over a scarred earth
that left jagged tracks
on soft, olive skin.

"Hey man," she pleads,
    "I wanna be loved,"
there in the night,
    hot and clammy
by the gate in the wall,
    paint peeling
from the bullet holes.
"I need somebody

love me."
"I love you," says the sailor,
    caressing her breast.
"I no think so," she hisses.
"I need somebody
        love me,
        no body,
            love me."

She embraces the sailor,
and death,
    on a sinking ship,
a sacrificial bier,
    in the murky water
of the river primeval.
        naked and clutching his watch,
        she drowns,
        forsaken by the sailor,
            swimming for shore.

"Come,
    yield me your body,"
the water gurgles and sighs,
"I'll embrace your cool flesh
    and give you time's balm
    to heal and refresh;
come lie 'neath me,
transfixed and transformed,
clutched tight
to death's bosom,
            safe from the storm."

An urchin

begging life,
    begs no more,
but beckons the sailor
    safe on the shore,
"Come,
    ride the dolphin's back,
    do not shrink
    from the deep,
come ... come here
with me to sleep."

AT A WINDOW

In the gray dark
of an October afternoon,
he stands by the window
and watches the rain
        streak the pane
and feels longing
and loneliness
        for the letter
                that never came.

On a bright-blue autumn day,
she watches the cat play
among the yellow leaves
        scuttering past
                in whirlwind gusts;
tail waving, back arched,
the cat dances on ballet toes,
        and she prays
                no one knows.

LOST: ON THE STATEN ISLAND FERRY

There, on an old worn seat, clean and cold,
I left it behind on the Staten Island Ferry—
after a walk on Wall Street,
a Saturday with darkness falling at four o'clock,
a wind chill of zero degrees,
a polar contrast to the heat, mosquitoes, and fear
      I had known only days before.
The cold, cold wind I remember,
but I can't remember
      what she said,
staring past me
at dusk settling over the water
      or perhaps at her reflection in the window.
She wore a bright red coat with gray fur at her neck
      and at her throat;
I wore padded gabardine,
      smooth and faded with age and use.
Did she wear a scarf, a hat? Did I?

It ended there, on the ferry sliding
through the black water of the harbor.
I can't remember what she said.
But what she said was true,
      truer than most words between lovers;
honest, confessional, expiatory,
      perhaps even pleading.

What she wanted, I do not know—
      to clear something away like the banked snow,
          icy and dirty on Broadway.

To this city I was a stranger, an explorer,
      on the Staten Island Ferry,
      going nowhere and back.
Whatever it was she said,
I looked out the window
      at the dusk turning night over the black water,
the lights, the statue and the lights not sparkling
         but dully glowing in the dusk.
I can't remember what she said.

The ferry entered the slip,
      and we exited through the gate
      (the only passengers coming back to the city,
         maybe a worker or two,
         the only fools wandering
            through ice-cold canyons at Saturday
      dusk because I wanted to ride
the Staten Island Ferry,
      no other goal than to ride the ferry,
         a frigid hour before sunset,
            under a sunless milk sky
            that turned to soot
               then faded to black)
and I ate the apple that she gave me.

Who knew the City could be so empty,
         so solitary.
Sitting there on the ancient wooden benches,
worn, scarred,

        new, newer now,
not seeing the statue or the skyline as she spoke,
only hearing her tell me
and feeling the frisson of despair
that wouldn't go away.
Only gray skies and no sunset to watch,
and the black night when we walked the icy streets
to the subway,
        Battery Park or somewhere near.
I was a stranger, I didn't know my way;
and what she said changed everything,
        the wages of blunt honesty,
two strangers on the Staten Island Ferry
going their separate ways.

FROM WHENCE WE CAME

From whence we came,
to where we go
we do not know,
nor should we care
except for fear.

When ice
coats the trees,
where do the doves flee?
And my mind,
where does it fly
when I have forgotten
what it was
that I forgot
and cannot remember
what I know,
and no longer see
what I have seen?

My friends,
they fall out
one by one
until I think
that we are none.

AFTER WE ARE DEAD

After we are dead
Throw out the papers
And spend all the cash.
The memories
      are ours,
           not yours;
They ended
      with the lapse,
           of that final,
                pulsing synapse,
Shredded and torn,
      blasted and shorn,
Leaves that faded
      and fell
           and decayed
Like all before
From Nebuchadnezzar,
      to Christian Dior.

So throw out the papers
And spend all the cash;
Our memories
      are now
           naught but trash.

A book of rhymes,
You can save,
      a doll
      or a toy,

That letter you scribbled
     on lined notepaper
          in deepest regret
For ripping curtains off the wall
     and tossing your mattress on the floor,
Til your progeny
Shall throw out your papers
And spend all your cash.

But wait!
Along the way
Raise a glass or two
     or three
          to me
And to you,

And have a fillet
     with a nice
          Beaujolais.
For a joy it was
     to be,
          to hear,
               to see,
Have been,
     lived free,
Breathed, walked,
     and run,
And all that censored fun.
Depressions,
     we savored
          and wallowed in,
And despair,
Could not compare
     to what is not,
Or pain endured,
     for when it passes,

And fear,
  for when it has fled
    once we are dead.

Life was good,
  and after ain't bad;
It was the dying we hated,
But when done,
  was done.

So throw out the papers
  and junk the old cars,
Rip up the photographs
  and sell the manse,
All that is there
  is done,
    the memories but dust.
And us?
We're nothing now,
That shall not fade
  and pass,
    along with tears
      and sorrows
       and gas.

So celebrate
  and procreate
What is, was, will be,
  for evermore:
An unseen adventure,
  an open door,
The drawing of straws,
  the roll of the dice
    by relict gods
      uncaring of odds.

And whatever you do
Before you're dead
Tell 'em all
      to throw out your papers
And spend all the cash
For there's
      nothing here
         that lasts.

A DREAM

A dream
of dark rooms and dusty stairways
dimly lit by the sun
in the afternoon.

A face unseen,
a voice unheard,
not just a dream,
a hint of presence,
lingering
like a breath (on a pane)
or a brushing past
and touching.

Someone near,
but not there,
I have known and touched,
but unknown and untouched,
someone passing
in a dream.

RETIREMENT

Each day,
I wend
      my way
           from café latte
    at matins
    to wine
at evensong.

THE JANITOR (CIRCA 1956)

Gray cement floors,
a smell of coal dust and a blazing fire
     from shovels of anthracite
     fueling yellow flames
     in a huge iron gray furnace—
through a door giving onto
the verisimilitude of hell
to my ten-year-old mind,
(confusing the poems still),
Dangerous Dan Magee
     stares out at me.
The warmth spreads
after the furnace door is shut;
and my father reads
the *Record & Landmark*
in a corner away from the fire's roar,
     under an overhead lamp
         (that dangles from a high ceiling
         crisscrossed with pipes)
casting down a circle of white light
that does not penetrate the far corners,
or go around the columns
or dilute their long shadows.

I sit on a rickety straight-back chair
     that once graced an office

and faced the face of authority,
while he leans back in an old swivel chair
        with bent wheels and worn seat pad,
        his feet propped up on a discarded desk.
Reading glasses glinting in the light,
        he stretches the paper wide
        with both hands in front of him.

Growing tired of looking at photographs
in *Life* and *Look* and *National Geographics*
intended for persons moved or dead or nonexistent
and relegated to the dead-letter box by the wall,
I wander to the elevator with its brass trim
        and scuffed checkerboard floor,
down the marble halls with their marble floors,
floors my father has swept and mopped and waxed,
through heavy wooden doors into restrooms
with toilets and sinks he's cleaned,
toilet paper and towel dispensers he's filled,
creeping into offices with swept-clean wooden floors,
light gleaming in the transoms,
        as I explore;
to the courtroom with its huge oak, swinging doors,
        yielding to my ten-year-old hands and shoulder,
        revealing the ebony
        of dais, tables, chairs, and railings,
        somber portraits,
        carved epigrams in cold granite,
        great seals in metal relief,
all dusted and polished;
        and shiny gold spittoons,
        reflecting slivers of light,
scrubbed and burnished

by my father
in his faded gray work pants and shirt,
the courtroom made ready
for the morning onslaught
      of judges and lawyers in pinstripe suits,
      prisoners, litigants,
      bailiffs, clerks, jurors, and spectators,
the court made ready for justice
by my father, the janitor,
whom I silently watch,
      still,
in the basement shadows,
work done for the night,
reading about events and people,
only history now,
this brief moment in time,
the two of us, soaking in the warmth,
breathing in the smell of burning coal
      and musty basement air,
content to live, to be,
as blood pumps through our veins
      and propels us on,
      actuates our minds
      in that space and time
there in the Post Office basement
      late at night before the end of his shift,
my father blowing on the edge of the paper
      to separate the pages
      and bend them to read the next words
      and more words after that
breathing, living,
      moving too quickly toward death.

DEPARTURES

Boarding trains, buses, and planes
        up steps, ramps, and inclines,
        on tracks, wheels and wings,
        steam,
            diesel exhaust,
                and roar.

People leaving,
     faces and arms and feet,
     voices and laughs and silence,
     tears and sadness
        and gladness.

Bags, coats, hats,
     briefcases and diapers,
     paper, pen, computer, phone,
     newspapers, books,
        dolls, toys and games.

Work, leisure,
     duty, pleasure.
     Joy and fear,
        weariness
           and boredom.
     Impatience,
        dread,
           drugged,
             drunk.

Waiting, hurrying,

standing, walking, running,
      up steps,
down ramp,
      through aisle,
         over knees and feet;
           seat,
              sit,
                  sat,
                  sitting.

Going home,
      going away,
      going to work,
      going to school,
      going to play,
      meeting someone,
      leaving someone.

Alone in the crowd.

Alone.
Leaving.

Going to war?
Going to die?

Departing
         alone.

SUNRISE AT BOOT CAMP

We sit in the dark,
     clammy with sweat,
Backs against the barracks' wall,
     floors waxed,
     commodes cleaned,
Windows shining in a 60-watt glow;
Eyes unborn to the dawn,
     staring
     at rows of packs and rifles
     grounded between the wooden buildings.

The sky changes,
     light gray;
     A lone pine tree struggles
Out of the sandy soil
That bears ghost prints
     of men marching to wars,
     Strides of those who came this way before.

Oh shit!
I forgot to fill my canteen,
     and the sinks are washed and clean.

High wisps of rose clouds,
     and I yearn to be free,
No more to hear the bone-death rattle of dog tags,
     the clang of metal wall lockers in the dark,
No more to taste the dust and hear the rasping orders
     that mean nothing to me.

Last week in the field, after chow,
The quiet kid from Indiana received a letter from his wife
      and slit his wrists with a P-38 army can opener;
Fifty push-ups and blood seeping through the bandages.
"You fail, you're fucked!" yells the drill sergeant.

The sun's slanting rays rest on the top of the pine.
"Fall in," the voice calls;
Not moving, I dream
      of different places and better times,
Of your body
      breaking the sparkling surface of the water.

ON GOING TO WAR

They are alone,
      together in the kitchen;
He paces behind her,
Then stops in the shadows.

Beyond her white hair,
      bent over the sink,
The uncovered windows
      frame black holes
      into the night.

"Mother, I go December first,"
      he says.

The light in the hall is dim,
The television stands blank and dark,
      a reflective eye behind him.
There is no sound
      except the ticking of the clock
      on the wall.

Her eyes are vacant,
And the wrinkles seem deeper,
      but she doesn't cry.
She says nothing,
Just turns away
      and looks
      out the window,
      into the night,
Dropping the ragged dish towel

by her side,
An old woman
        thinking that death
        would be kinder.

TEACH YOUR CHILDREN WELL

The things I told my children when they were young:
dinosaurs, trilobites, horseshoe crabs, fossils,
Uncle Scrooge, Uncle Remus, Uncle Wiggily,
planets, galaxies, protons, electrons, neutrinos,
the big bang, black holes,
Blackbeard, Billy the Kid,
amoeba, protozoa,
Diogenes' lantern, Plato's cave,
American slavery, the Holocaust,
"The Beast in the Jungle,"
Bucephalus, Alexander the Great,
the speed of light, my warped theory of relativity,
never assume anything,
species extinction—
and my son asked, "when will humans go extinct?"
he said, while I was changing clothes after work;
"Dad, when's it going to end?"
He was four or five, I think.
And I answered, "when's what going to end?"
"When's it *all* going to end?" he asked.
He was sitting, spindly legs crossed,
in the center of the bed.
"I don't want to die," he said.

LETTER HOME

Yesterday,
just before sunset,
the short, round cook,
          who looks like Lou Costello,
tried to kill Captain Midnight
with an M-16.

They carried him off,
          the little doughboy cook,
          in his dirty white t-shirt,
yelling, crying, handcuffed,
and there were bullet holes
          in the ceiling.

How's the weather now?
It's spring, isn't it?
But I guess not
since it's still February.
          I keep forgetting
          because it's always hot here.
But I miss mowing the grass,
the smell of wild onions
after they've been cut.

The Lou Costello cook is kept in a cell,
Eight-by-eight, with only a cot and a bucket.

He said, "Don't move."
I ran.

A DANGEROUS WORLD

To see the world through another's eyes
is a dangerous thing:
the loneliness of a widowed mother
as the child slips away,
the desperation of a child
when a parent blinks out
or flees
or just doesn't understand.

To own their sorrows
and know their secrets
is despair and fear.

How can we care
      if we do not know?
How can we know
      if we do not see,
            when we avert our eyes,
Since we are not ...
      we are not?

I am not a refugee in a leaky boat,
      waiting to sink;
I am not hungry,
      rooting through garbage;
I am not black or brown
      living in a ghetto forsaken by hope;
I am not an unwanted immigrant
      seeking a better life;
I am not an angry white man

watching Fox News;
I am not a black man
    fleeing a uniform;
I am not a cop's spouse
    starting at each knock on the door;
I am not a single mother
    watching her child off to school;
I am not a soldier
    facing an unseen enemy;
I am not a veiled bride
    seeing death rain from the sky;
I am not a breast cancer survivor
    facing a mirror;

I am not disabled,
    struggling through a door;
I am not a debt-ridden farmer,
    tilling dead fields;
I am not oppressed for my religion or race;
I am not gay afraid to come out;
I am not a teenage girl pregnant and alone;
I am not poor and working two jobs;
I am not homeless.
Homeless ...

He watches the cars
    go past,
and the drivers, stopped,
staring at anything but him—
    gaunt, wasted,
    time and drink and fate ravaged—
and his cardboard sign
    with its crayon-scrawled letters
    that ask for ...
and we look away
or hand a folded bill out the window
and drive on,

forgetting,
denying,
that we have seen ourselves
in the rear-view mirror,
as he waves farewell
          with a raised
                    middle finger.

WAR OF THE MARTINS AND SPARROWS

In my side yard, there's a birdhouse we put up
      for purple martins.
We like hearing them chatter and burble,
      seeing them soar and swoop and
      land like fighter jets on an aircraft carrier.
The sparrows came; they built a nest,
      then two martins returned from South America
      and they built a nest, side-by-side with the sparrows.
Now it looks like there are two sparrow nests,
      one on each side of the house,
      and both sparrows and martins have cropped,
      and there are birds all over the house,
      both house sparrows and purple martins.
They fight all the time,
      on the porches, even inside one of the holes with
      feathers poking out,
      these two tribes of ex-dinosaurs.
Why can't they live like humans, in peace and harmony?
There's plenty of room for all,
      twelve holes, six to a side, and two floors.
But the agile and musical purple martin
      (not so pretty a specimen)
      and the common sparrow
      (the male, quite striking when seen up close,
      only chirps and chirps
      and tenaciously holds his ground—
      and breeds prolifically),
      they, the martins and sparrows,
      waste their time and energy fighting over

        this one house
        we bought just for the martins.
And there's danger to both:
        the hawk giving its piercing call above,
        the snake that coiled its way up the pole at my
        former house
        and cleaned out the martin nests
        and not even the sparrows would come back.
If they had complex brains and thought and religion,
        each tribe would probably justify its claim to the
        house
        by some divine right,
        a gift from some god
        for who knows what reason,
        and rationalize their instinctive struggle
        for nesting turf and survival
        by some mystical, mythical divine dispensation.
But this god, who put up the house for the martins
        and wanted the martins to come,
        and they did come,
        wishes they'd all just shut up the infernal racket
        and share the damn house.

A RISING TIDE

I feel the tide rising,
    I see faces all around,
    different shapes
        and shades of hair
            and colors of skin.

In a Budapest museum, homage is paid to those who fled
    —inventors, theorists, thinkers
    —artists, musicians, writers
Welcomed in another place,
    and what they brought with them:
        television, laser, computer,
            paint, piano, and pen,
The HY-DRO-GEN BOMB,
    and the eighth dimension unstrung.

They, the celebrated,
    are but the froth,
    the effervescence
        of the movement of peoples,
    Not the essence.

Yet another wave comes—
    short, dark men,
        digging, hammering, sweating, straining,
    building houses, mending roofs.
Imagine their struggles, their strivings,

their sorrows, their fears,
                their loneliness
Now that they are here.

Small dark women with straight black hair
        push strollers with blond, blue-eyed babies
        and stop in the park to talk in a lyrical tongue,
        staving off loneliness and fear of what will come,
What will happen tomorrow—here.

There is a past—for them and for this place,
                of those welcomed and those turned away
                        —some into the maw of their enemies;
A past of some dragged here in chains;
A past of all those who came any way they could.
I am part of it—
        a great movement of peoples—
        peripatetic tribes,
                seekers of freedom or fortune,
        refugees from evils,
                or responsibilities;
Some who prospered, some who did not;
All lived and died, loved and sorrowed,
        in this new place.

I see the tide rising,
        and I welcome it,
I go with it in exultation and praise:
WE are the tide,
        we are the tide, rising,
                every one of us.

As we followed others,
        so too
                shall others follow us
                        to these shores,
A rising tide

until death comes
>   and sweeps us aside,
leaving this ground we walk
and the air we breathe
>   to others
>   who follow,
Each and every one,
>   rising, ebbing, flowing,
>   like the tide.

RUMINATIONS
(RANDOM THOUGHTS STRUNG TOGETHER)

The weeks roll by like boxcars on a passing freight
      at a railroad crossing in a west Texas town—
         a main street full of empty stores
            and gray, limestone buildings
            that once held money and
            beds for those who had it.
It's neither good nor bad;
it's just the way it is
until the train is gone
and you cross over to the other side of the tracks.
The sun rises, the sun sets.

In the attic of the house my father built,
I found a battered trunk with a broken lock and bent
latches,
faded to gray by fleeting time—
      empty,
except for a large American flag
      folded in a neat triangle.
Curious, wondering why it was there,
I spread it out over a long wooden table
      my father had made years before,
and after examining the heavy fabric and still-bright
colors
in dust-filled light from the attic windows,
refolded it in a "cocked hat" shown in my Scouts'
Handbook,
      and replaced it in the trunk,

where it remained until my father's generation was
gone,
the house was sold,
     and the flag was lost.

In the hurricane's howling winds,
     windows and doors shake and creak,
while ancient oaks sway and bend
             and break,
flinging tired limbs onto houses
     until the storm passes
     and the sun shines again.

A lightning bolt strikes the tall pine by the house,
punching a hole through the wall,
     and into a water pipe,
     flooding the room below.
The pine, eighty rings or more,
     survives,
     still tall and straight and green,
     until lightning strikes again,
punching a hole in wall and pipe,
     flooding the room below.
The first was a warning, the second punishment
     for not heeding the first,
     believing the sun shall always rise
     and lightning never strikes twice.

In the far north-Atlantic, a warship seeks safe harbor
     in a sheltered cove,
     protected from a raging winter storm,
         but savage waves still heave and surge,
            towering high over steel hull
            and deck,
            driving the ship onto rocks
            near shore,

            sending hundreds of sailors (and my Uncle
            Jim)
            to a swift, icy death,
                victims not of war but of human
                error,
        left to lie in foreign graves 'til war's end,
        returned home in steel-encased boxes
        not to be opened.
Despite human tragedy and despair,
the sun shall rise and set
until it does so nevermore.

Have you ever seen white-wing doves mate?
An elaborate billing and cooing
and rubbing together of wings,
side by side;
and one, the female I guess,
shivers and shudders all over,
then the male hops on top.
It's over in seconds,
but it does the trick
'cause doves fill the live oaks out back
and cover the ground beneath
       with white splotches.

Like an old snake, I live out my life
from meal to meal,
engorged and flatulent
until the bulge settles and I eat again
in a headlong rush to the end.
Or is it only an idle stroll to the precipice?
For I have no answers to any of it,
only that the sun rises and the sun sets.

My only regrets
are for time wasted
and opportunities squandered,

none to do with wealth or power
or even success—except in bed.

After the kids came along,
we finally donned pajamas
and something was lost
and gone forever,
but from life I have learned
in all things there is symmetry
even as it seems there is none.

We can never go back again,
and so as the sun rises, the sun sets.
At one end of the tunnel
there is light, at the other
the mystery of night.

TWENTY-SIX POEMS: PUBLICATION INDEX

I Am Not a Poet
[Published in *Our Poetica*, Cathexis Northwest Press, 2019]

Why Did Hemingway Kill Himself?
[Published in *Sheila-Na-Gig* online, Summer 2017]

The Wench Is Dead
[Published in *Untold Stories, An Anthology*, Military Writers Society of America 2021]

Vinh Long at Dusk
[Published in *Dream Machinery*, Issue 2, May 1994]

The Runner

White Guilt
[Published in *The Athena Review*, Issue 1, January 2020]

On Growing Old and Discovering Truth
[Published in *Burningword Literary Journal*, Issue 91, July 2019]

We Were in the Water Then

In the End?

War's Child
[Published in *Untold Stories, An Anthology*, Military Writers Society of America 2021]

At a Window

Lost: On the Staten Island Ferry
[Published in *Sheila-Na-Gig* online, Summer 2017]

From Whence We Came

After We Are Dead
[Published in *Burningword Literary Journal*, Issue 93, January 2020]

A Dream
[Published in *Dream Machinery*, Issue #2, May 1994]

Retirement

The Janitor

Departures
Published in *Untold Stories, An Anthology*, Military Writers Society of America 2021]

Sunrise at Boot Camp
[Published in *Untold Stories, An Anthology*, Military Writers Society of America 2021]

On Going to War
[Published in *Untold Stories, An Anthology*, Military Writers Society of America 2021]

Teach Your Children Well

Letter Home
Published in *Untold Stories, An Anthology*, Military Writers Society of America 2021]

A Dangerous World
[Published in *Out of Many, One*, Houston Writers Guild Anthology 2017]

War of the Martins and Sparrows
[Published in *Out of Many, One*, Houston Writers Guild Anthology 2017]

A Rising Tide
[Published in *Out of Many, One*, Houston Writers Guild Anthology 2017]

Ruminations

Thank you so much for reading *Ruminations: Stories, Essays, and Poems*. If you've enjoyed the book, we would be grateful if you would post a review on the bookseller's website. Just a few words is all it takes!

Acknowledgments

I want to thank all who have read drafts of my writings over the years and, most recently, Tom Watts and Pam Fisher, who also wrote poetry in high school and read my poems even back then—most of which ended up on the cutting room floor. For the family history reflected in "The Poisoning," I am indebted to R.C. and Irene Clanton Black for sharing their research into the Bell family along with copies of the news clippings from the *Statesville Landmark* and documents from the coroner's inquest into the death of Thomas Smith Bell on August 9, 1888. A special thanks to Janis Wieland Dodson for saving a few of my letters from Vietnam, including one with the original draft of "Mick." And always my wife, June, who tries to decipher my writing, patiently proofs my work, and endeared herself to me by typing a law school brief early one morning as the sun rose to help me get a good grade in a Federal Courts seminar (because my writing was, allegedly, illegible).

Made in the USA
Coppell, TX
13 February 2024

28894873R00122